To J

with love U—

Victoria

September 2009

Always a Romance of Lemuria

The Lost Continent of the Pacific Ocean

Victoria Helen Turner

The story of a love which existed in a lost paradise when even Atlantis was a golden infant in the womb of the Future, a love which defied Time and Death itself, a love that was to last

AuthorHouse™
1663 Liberty Drive, Suite 200
Bloomington, IN 47403
www.authorhouse.com
Phone: 1-800-839-8640

© 2009 Victoria Helen Turner. All rights reserved.

No part of this book may be reproduced, stored in a retrieval system, or transmitted by any means without the written permission of the author.

First published by AuthorHouse 2/5/2009

ISBN: 978-1-4389-3332-0 (sc)

Printed in the United States of America
Bloomington, Indiana

This book is printed on acid-free paper.

'Yet love will dream and faith will trust,
Since He who knows our need is just,
That somehow, somewhere, meet we must.
Alas for him who never sees
The stars shine through his cypress trees!
Who hath not learned in hours of faith,
That truth to flesh and sense unknown,
That Life is ever lord of Death,
And Love can never lose its own!'

    AUTHOR UNKNOWN

This book is dedicated
To the Gifted and Beautiful
Star of Hollywood's Golden Era who inspired the
fictional character of
'Tristan Zennor' and who like 'Tristan' was taken before
his time, and so I dedicate this story to him with love
and admiration –
'Always'

And most of all to my beloved late mother, Ruth.

Contents

Part One	1
Part Two	105

Part One

Always
A Romance of Lemuria

PROLOGUE

Here also - he was always there - my beloved - the One Who Would Come, though I didn't always know he was beside me, that truelove never dies, for love is stronger than death – death is like a chasm which seems deep and dark and on one side is Life - physical life, and the other side is that other Life, which we call Death and the one who lives physically looks across the chasm at the one who we call dead and in spirit the hands are held, bridging the chasm, the clasp as strong and firm as Love itself, for love is stronger than that we call life or death. Nothing can break or end that love enshrined in that clasp, and the day comes when the living one must cross the chasm and be encircled by the arms of the beloved forever and ever through life and death, death and life - I know because I was there!

It is only that which we call life that I remember, it is not for us to see or remember the other side of the chasm, only to know it is there and is not the end, for we know from He who went and came back and is Love Itself. This is the law between all living things, human and animal... all love lives on even between a human and his beloved pet, even such a humble love as this, not only that between a man and a woman, though that is the most beautiful. Someone once said... "nothing is ever lost - it is only somewhere else..."

1990

Lunaflora Howard clipped together the latest pages of her historical novel, clean crisp paper freshly printed from her word processor, and gave a little sigh as she caught sight of the silver framed photograph beside her, a photo of a young man of breathtaking beauty, dark haired, whose brilliant thickly lashed black eyes seemed to smile into her dark blue ones across the thirty five years which separated them.

The usual stab of sadness went through her as she recalled that those beautiful eyes had been closed in death for thirty five years. Yet when she watched the films of Tristan Zennor, it seemed only yesterday that this incredibly handsome star with the most attractive voice and dramatic talent of his generation had laughed and clashed swords in so many first rate swashbuckling , historical adventure, and fantasy films, not to mention several serious modern dramatic films, for which he was awarded an Oscar. Then came the last film, that fateful autumn day in 1955, when he was making a fantasy film called 'Always', taken from a bestselling novel about the lost continent of Lemuria - for authenticity, he and his leading lady Lunaflora were in the sea, they were supposed to be drowning, it was the very last take, and it was their last moment, there was a sudden squall, a wave came and they were both drowned! The film world was stunned! What a waste! Only forty years old - and the woman they say he had loved gone with him - but how romantic... said some...

Lunaflora Howard held the copy of the novel in her hand, a very old copy, it was called 'Always - A Romance of Lemuria by Contessa Angelina Velucci. It had been a best seller in its day, at the end of the Victorian era. The kind of thing that appealed not only to readers of its day but to the epic making Hollywood of the nineteen fifties. It was the book that had cost Tristan Zennor and his leading lady, Lunaflora Wood, their lives. It had happened in Hawaii, where they had done much of the filming. They were flown back to Hollywood. They were buried together, she in her twenty eighth year, and over the grave alongside their deceased Hollywood contemporaries stood a beautiful stone angel with outstretched wings - and in Latin - a simple epitaph 'Omnia vincit amor', Love Conquers All.

Tristan Zennor had been married for the second time when he met Lunaflora, but it was already on the rocks. There were no children to mourn him, rumour had it that Lunaflora was having a baby at the time of her death - perhaps they planned to marry - now they would never know! Only his two sisters and two wives stood at the graveside together with many fellow actors and people of the film world - all who had loved or just liked this easy going and good natured young man who would never grow old.

Apart from his looks and talent and his reputation with the ladies, which equalled that of Errol Flynn, the young Tristan had a refinement and culture which made him stand out from many of his fellow actors. His first wife had been an intellectual German actress of great beauty and they had both had a love of great literature and beautiful music. They also shared a delightful sense of humour, but his many affairs had finally broken her heart. His second wife, Conchita, was a beautiful but rather empty headed small-time Spanish actress who had picked up the pieces after Marta Helman, the German wife had divorced him. In spite of his many love affairs he was an incurable romantic who seemed to be searching for that one person of whom both men and women always hoped would be waiting somewhere as Bing Crosby had sung 'Where the Blue of the Night meets the Gold of the Day.'

When Jean Marshall, the sexy but talented blonde actress, who had starred in many of his films withdrew from the film 'Always', as she was retiring to become a wife and mother, they were desperate to find a new leading lady. Every beautiful female star in Hollywood was considered, until a mysterious young woman, with the then ridiculous name of Lunaflora Wood, was noticed by Tristan himself among the extras. She was attractive rather than pretty with dreamy blue eyes and golden brown hair which as they say 'she could sit on'. She was completely bewitched by the attentions of this great star, who, at first only took her to the right parties and where they danced the night away. It was obvious to everyone that Lunaflora was desperately in love with the world's greatest romantic idol, and at last it looked as if Tristan also had found his truelove. The girl's past was mysterious, no-one seemed to know where she had come from. The only thing she would say was that she had been born in England, her mother had named her Lunaflora because as a young girl she had read the novel 'Always' and had decided to call her daughter after the heroine - who in the book, and later, in the film was called 'Moonflower', which though beautiful was rather farfetched for a modern name so 'Lunaflora' which means the same thing was the nearest she could get. It was either fate or coincidence that she was chosen to play the part of the very heroine she was named after - Moonflower - queen of Lemuria, with Tristan playing the part of Rama, the King of Lemuria!

Lunaflora Howard was named after the heroine and the actress, her mother had wanted to call her Moonflower, but her father thought the name too outlandish so it became Lunaflora. Her parents had been on their honeymoon when the two stars died, in fact, Lunaflora mused, she herself must have been conceived not long after for she was born in September of the following year! She had inherited her mother's admiration for Tristan Zennor and the film 'Always' in particular. It seemed to hold some meaning for her - she had been in love with Tristan Zennor since childhood and had an uncanny resemblance to the actress Lunaflora Wood, same long golden brown hair and dreamy blue eyes. Now at thirty four, single and a successful writer of romantic historical novels, she was still in love with Tristan Zennor. She'd had her share of boyfriends, was once even engaged - but it didn't work out - all the men she dated had dark good looks but not quite like... Tristan Zennor. Then there was the ring... two years before she had gone to an auction where Hollywood memorabilia was being auctioned off for charity. She caught sight of one of the items. It was a silver ring surmounted by a large milky opal, surrounded by smaller opals - in fact it was designed in the shape of a flower. One of the auctioneers noted her interest:

"Unusual - isn't it," he remarked. She looked at him, a man in his early sixties.

"Yes, it is..." the stone seemed to sparkle at her and she was drawn to it as if hypnotized.

"It is the ring that Tristan Zennor gave to the woman who died with him," said the man, "a love token I suppose, it's meant to be a moonflower - if you know the story of course, you're rather young to know..." Lunaflora's heart was thudding...

"Yes - I do know - I might bid for it," she said.

She did bid for it - a lot of people were interested, but she went as high as she dared and she left the auction room with the ring on the third finger of her left hand - it might have been made for her and it was then that it all began....

Chapter One

'Tell me where all past times are!' - Donne

That ring was essentially a birthday present from her mother. Lunaflora had just turned thirty four. Her father had died when she was two years old, and her mother had returned home to live with her parents. Lunaflora's grandmother had cared for the child while her mother went out to work. It was hard in the late fifties and early sixties bringing up a child on one's own. Lunaflora was fascinated from a child with the world of films and theatre, she also loved books. Her first love then, however, apart from Tristan Zennor, was ballet. From the age of ten to eighteen, she had trained for ballet; she had all the necessary qualities except the toughness and stamina. She could teach ballet she was told, but she wanted to be on the stage, so if not ballet, there was acting. She was accepted for drama school, but grants for drama school were few and far between. So by day she pounded a typewriter, her mother had seen that she had taken a secretarial course while still at school, and by night, five nights a week and on Saturday she attended drama classes.

She was soon given the leading parts in many of the school productions, the first in a play about Abraham

Lincoln; she remembered that one because at first she could only manage a Southern belle accent. Then she played the part of the old maid in 'The Corn is Green', she even appeared in an amateur film with an ancient history theme, she was a Babylonian hand- maid in an orgy scene. Then the triumph of her brief dramatic career was the leading part in 'Stage Door' which had once been filmed with the great Katherine Hepburn. The Principal of the drama school told Lunaflora that she had great talent that she would probably go far in even in such an overcrowded profession as acting. She had looks, talent and the additional skills of being able to dance, play the piano and sing.

To this day she never really knew why she left, it wasn't the male student with his unwelcome attentions, she was used to that, she had plenty of attention from the men she met, but she never seemed to meet the right one. She was sometimes quiet, but not shy and she could talk with anybody. It was hard to remember the reason she had left. Perhaps the kind of films they were making in the seventies did not appeal to her, or the plays either - mainly kitchen sink drivel! She'd cut her teeth on the golden era of Hollywood and British films, not to mention television. What child of her generation had not avidly watched the handsome Richard Greene in Robin Hood? The films and plays of the seventies and late sixties were not all bad - what about 'Dr Zhivago' or 'Far from the Madding Crowd' - to name a few and there were good ones in the eighties too - romance was returning! Well, she had left drama school, which she sometimes regretted. She went back to the office, joined a local group of young people involved with politics where she met a young man who dented her heart but did not break it! She had always read widely - so she took advantage of the fairly new Open University and after six years obtained a degree - a Bachelor of Arts Degree no less, with the emphasis on English Literature and Drama. She had always written stories from childhood and while studying for her degree had joined a local writers group, mainly made up of little old ladies and retired brigadiers but gradually a few younger people had joined. She also found time to appear in some amateur dramatic and operatic performances, so she was fairly content - or was she? She wrote short historical stories for her writer's group, together with a little poetry, children's stuff and a few one act plays. She won cups in many of their competitions and over the years became Chairman of the group. She had always liked fantasy and one day began a fantasy novel set long ago before history. She had to admit to herself that the book and the later film with Tristan Zennor had to some extent been the inspiration, but after two years, her novel, 'When the Silver Moon was Gold' was finished. She had had some short stories on her local radio, but this was her first novel, so she showed it to her Open University tutor. He read it and thought it was very good, he said he would show it to a literary agent friend of his. The agent took her on and from then on she didn't look back. Her first novel was a bestseller; another followed, together with some historical romances - all best sellers! Lunaflora Howard was a household name - her first novel was going to be turned into a Hollywood film, it was this event that happened after she had bought the ring! Her agent 'phoned her and told her that the famous Hollywood film company, one of the few famous names still operating, namely 'Romulus 2000' was interested in making her first novel into a fantasy film. She was overjoyed, in fact to make a pun, she was over the moon, and now in two weeks' time she was off to Hollywood to advise on certain points and meet the stars and if she wished, watch some of the film being shot. The male part was being played by Miller Gilbert and the female by Sophia Dixon, they weren't bad looking as modern stars went, in fact Miller Gilbert had surprised everyone with some of his recent historical epics, he'd turned out a very good actor!

It wasn't these people Lunaflora was eager to meet; her heart had missed a beat when she had realized that

Romulus 2000 was the studio of which Tristan Zennor had been a star!

Having always had a weakness for actors, especially ones who resembled the dead star, Lunaflora had met a former actor, not a star but someone who very nearly did break her heart, but she recovered and returned to her first love. Yes, fantastic as it seemed, this long dead star was her love... now she was going to Hollywood... the dreams began... one minute she was in a tropical jungle where huge moonflower blossoms, such as she had never seen before, but which smelt like exotic violets, filled her senses and she was being kissed senseless by the man she had only seen in dreams or on the screen, it seemed a time before time... there was a silence except for birdsong that she had never heard on earth, then the same scene was on a film set, the flowers were imitation, only the look in those beautiful black eyes so near her own seemed to say 'I adore you' - and that was real! She became aware that she was dressed in an elaborate costume of a long flared gown, silver grey, and covered with hundreds of miniatures of those same moonflower blossoms the scent of which a moment ago had overpowered her with its sensuality mixed with that of the overpower exciting sensuality of the vibrant young man who held her in lightly tanned arms, whose fantastic golden costume was heightened by the sparkle of gold dust on his finely shaped limbs. On her own hair she wore a garland of those same moonflowers and she unconsciously put up a hand to touch the slightly waving black hair of this man of whom she had waited for so long. Above his dark eyebrows, a golden band encircled his head, blazing red golden fire, white hot as it met her moonflowers, mingling into a mutual fountain of passion as his lips once more descended and a voice called 'Cut' - and she woke up!

The harsh early morning light, darkening to the dreary grey of gathering rainclouds, brought Lunaflora completely out of the lovely dream. She always slept with the curtains drawn back a little. On moonlit summer nights, she liked the silvery radiance shining like a soft spotlight through her bedroom window, sometimes adding stars to the silver framed photo of her heart's desire on top of her small piano.

All the love songs she had ever heard seemed to echo through those dreams - songs of her mother's and grandmother's youth - 'I'll be loving you - always,' and an even older one that had been in the most successful operetta of the Victorian era - people were singing it when her great grand-mother was just born! So popular was the melody, it was a frequently played piece in theatre, ballroom and drawing rooms right into the 20th century. Sometimes it seemed as if it might have been written just for her - it was called 'The Dream',- 'I dreamt that I dwelt in marble halls with vassals and serfs at my side - and that you loved me still' - the song had outlasted the operetta 'The Bohemian Girl', apart from a film version - still obtainable, made partly into comedy but keeping much of the lovely music with of all people - Laurel and Hardy, and in a small part an actress who was the victim of one of Hollywood's greatest murder mysteries - Thelma Todd!"

Yes, sometimes Lunaflora seemed to recall marble halls and the beautiful young man in whose arms she lay, whispering words of some forgotten tongue - not English - yet which were beautiful and which she could understand, and all the beauty of the world, of all ages and all time seemed to surround them both like a golden mist until .it penetrated them both as they made love, not just visual beauty or the beauty of the senses, though these were a part of it, but of music – love itself - and its handmaidens - joy, loyalty, honour, truth, decency, part of the divine pattern of love and understanding, and a kind of lovely compassion of union which neither time nor death could destroy - part of life and of eternity!

Great vines twisted around those pale marble columns, with enormous moonflower blossoms... it gave the columns the effect of flowers twisted around the beautiful braids of some gorgeous giantess, and statues of such beautiful women or perhaps goddesses stood or reclined between those columns, regarding the lovers with secret impersonal smiles concealed in their lowered eyes... the only live creature apart from themselves was a lemur with a black face and amber eyes, also regarding them where it perched, halfway up a column, its head leaning against a Moonflower... Lunaflora opened her eyes, she could still see the lemur, a beautiful but stuffed toy one on her twentieth century divan bed... a poem came to her... if we had world enough and time... this coyness lady would be no crime... perhaps it was Andrew Marvell... what did it matter... what did anything matter... when her dream lover had vanished with the deep dark mystery of night!

Chapter Two

Lunaflora was making travel arrangements; or rather her agent was to fly to Los Angeles and Hollywood. They were sitting in the lounge of Lunaflora's house, or rather large cottage near the small Somerset town of Glastonbury. Apart from a daily housekeeper, she lived alone; her mother had re-married long ago and lived in New Zealand. They sat either side of the coffee table, silent for the moment, apart from the odd clink of teacups, and the purr of Lunaflora's large tabby cat, Caruso, named after the legendary tenor, who sat, with paws stretched out, looking like, and as inscrutable as the Sphinx as he gazed as was his mistress and Lucy, the agent, through the window at the mysterious Tor rising up through the mist – "the mist of time", said Lunaflora, thinking aloud, and studying her moonflower ring.

Lucy's eyes too, studied the ring.

"The mist of time," she repeated. She knew of Lunaflora's obsession with Tristan Zennor.

"You know," she said, putting her cup on the table, "I've heard there's one of those white witches, or whatever they are called, just moved into Glastonbury, she's a clairvoyant, I hear she's very good, why don't you consult her?"

"But why?" said Lunaflora, "how could she help?" Lucy shrugged.

"I don't know, but you never know, it might be worth a try."

A week or two later, only a few weeks away from her trip to Hollywood, Lunaflora and Lucy went to the Bristol Coliseum to see a revival of J M Barrie's 'Mary Rose' by a local theatre company. It was a beautiful old theatre, the red and gold of the auditorium had been restored some years previously and it was now much as it was when... it was strange, Lunaflora had never been to this theatre before, yet it seemed familiar. She was not a native of the West Country, so no childhood treat had been spent here that she had forgotten. Perhaps it was the fact that she knew – Tristan Zennor - not perhaps remembered, by many people - had appeared on this very stage in another Barrie play - 'Dear Brutus', in the part of the father of the 'Dream Daughter – Margaret'. It was the last but one stop of the only touring play he had ever appeared in on a Bristol stage. The tour had opened in London and gone up to Scotland - from there to Bristol, and ending in Dublin. During his week in Bristol he - it was the May of 1953, he had found time to make a flying visit, literally, as he was a pilot, to the country of his ancestors - Cornwall - and the Scilly Isles where his father, a matinee idol of his day, and a friend of the great Irving, had been born. Perhaps his father, also called Tristan, had been named after the legendary Tristan of Lyonesse, of which the Scilly Isles, it was said, had once been a part, also the Tristan who had loved Isolda, Queen of Ireland, their love too had been tragic!

After the play was over, Lunaflora went to the Manager's Office to ask if there was anyone who remembered that long ago appearance of Tristan Zennor.

"See Rose," the Manager said, "she's been here fifty years, she started, here as a 14 year old cashier in the Box Office. I've heard of Tristan Zennor, but he's a bit before my time, although I've seen his films on TV. Rose is our archivist and there's a small museum in the basement." Down a steep flight of stairs went Lunaflora, smelling that indefinable smell of backstage in old theatres, a mixture of dust, wood and greasepaint and generations of the great, and she also had a distinct feeling of 'I've been here before'. Rose was a smiling, smartly dressed woman, looking much younger than a person of around sixty four.

"Oh my dear," she said, "this theatre is like my home, it is my home."

"Do you remember when the great Hollywood screen star Tristan Zennor was here?" asked Lunaflora.

"Tristan Zennor - oh yes - I remember - who could possibly forget him? - They had to bring in policemen to hold back the hundreds of screaming girls and women waiting for him - he was an absolute smasher! - had the most beautiful eyes and smile I've ever seen - and there was no side on him - stood, for an hour writing autographs the day he arrived for rehearsal. Of course, stars had real looks in those days, not like the ugly, scruffy, vulgar louts they scream after today. Tristan Zennor was a gentleman but he had an eye for the ladies." For a moment Lunaflora saw in the almost elderly woman the pretty girl she must once have been - she was still good looking.

"I was the manager's private secretary then," she continued, "but used to help out generally, and although I wouldn't tell this to anybody - well I was in the room where they stored old props, scenery and so on, and like most girls of my generation was absolutely hypnotised by Tristan Zennor - in his films he was stunning - but in real life, and with that beautiful voice of his, American and yet with an almost English refinement about it - well anyway," she said, looking a bit pink, "I was in the storeroom, getting a few things for the stage manager, when the door opened behind me, and there was Tristan with that wonderful but rather wicked smile - I knew his reputation - and I knew what to expect, he wasn't a heartless seducer like some of his fellow stars, it was rather that women seduced him, but this time he did chase me and there was a rather old but convenient couch in that storeroom – and he turned the key in the lock, and let's say I didn't put up much resistance - two months later I married my fiancé, earlier than planned, and the twins, Susan and David, now both married with children of their own, do not resemble my late husband or indeed myself..." Lunaflora's head shot up.

"Are you saying...?"

"It's possible, but no-one ever has or will know." Lunaflora smiled.

"I wouldn't tell - he was no angel." The other woman moved to a display, "here are some old publicity posters and a few photos, you know, it's a funny thing, but you remind me of the girl who played 'Margaret' in the play with him. She came, after the incident with me; she stepped in when the actress playing the part originally was rushed to hospital with appendicitis. It's funny... he seemed to change when she came, he couldn't take his eyes off her... he must have really fallen for her, she had your beautiful hair and eyes... the resemblance is quite remarkable. He took her back to Hollywood with him you know... she was the one who starred with him in that last film and who died with him."

"Lunaflora – it's my name as well, I was called after her, but I never knew they met here!"

Always a Romance of Lemuria

"Your resemblance to her is uncanny," the woman Rose said, "well just one of those things I suppose." Lunaflora looked at a faded photo of the company taken on the last night, at the party after the performance; there was Tristan, an arm around the girl who might have been herself!

"After the revelation at the theatre, Lunaflora decided to find out a little more about her namesake. In the few biographies of Tristan Zennor, there was very little about her - she seemed to have come from nowhere. After another talk by 'phone with the Woman Rose at the theatre, she managed to find out that the first Lunaflora had been born in a village not far from Stratford-upon-Avon in 1930. Her father had been a musician in the variety and musical side of the theatre, her mother, apart from being an avid reader was a semi-successful writer of romances herself. As a child the first Lunaflora saw many of the plays at Stratford and at the age of sixteen, she went to a London drama school, then into repertory in various parts of the country, graduating to leading ladies and finally being taken on by the Bristol Coliseum as a last minute replacement for the part of Margaret in 'Dear Brutus' in which Tristan Zennor was appearing on a tour. By a strange coincidence, as a small child, she had seen the film star's father at Stratford playing the part of

Prospero in 'The Tempest' - not very long after he had died of a heart attack - only in his sixties.

All this Lunaflora was able to find out from the London drama school where the retired secretary had been a student and friend of the first Lunaflora. The woman sent all the information in a long letter to Lunaflora after she had written to the elderly woman on obtaining her address from the still existing drama school. She had explained her interest in the film actor and how she had been named after the book and his leading lady in the film and in life. After Tristan had taken the girl to Hollywood, the trail went cold, the friend said she lost contact with the lady after she met Tristan and only heard of her again when she appeared in the film and was so tragically drowned with her lover. The friend did write that the actress's parents had died while the girl was a student and there were no relatives.

That was all Lunaflora could find out about her namesake and mirror image. Then in the last few days before she was due to fly Hollywood, she went to visit the clairvoyant that Lucy had mentioned. She drove into Glastonbury, parked near the abbey and entered an ancient building off the High Street and climbed a steep, creaking staircase and knocked on the door marked 'Madam Selma'. A deep but feminine voice called to her to enter. She opened the door and saw a woman in late middle age; she was dressed in a long green shift with floating sleeves. Her black hair was parted in the centre and pulled back into a severe Spanish bun. Clanking green coloured miniature chandeliers dangled from her ears. Though she vaguely resembled Madam Arcati in 'Blithe Spirit', Lunaflora's silent amusement was checked as she looked into the woman's deep set dark eyes.

"Sit down, my dear," she said. The girl sat down. "Don't tell me anything - just give me your ring."

"My ring?" said Lunaflora, puzzled.

"Yes, your ring." She drew the moonflower ring from her finger... it seemed to glow in the darkened room. The woman stared at it, then held it in her hands and closed her eyes.

"I seem to see two ages entwined as tightly as the lovers who are at the heart of them. The two ages touch on the present age, which is really the end of the second age. You, the owner of the ring are one of the lovers... you have always been the owner of the ring... since you were given it by your beloved in a time before time... you always had the same name... Moonflower, like the stone in the ring. Your lover is not with you now, not physically, but he was, is and will be with you - always! In that time before time I see you... you are a queen, yet only a small child still, sitting on a great golden throne. The throne is studded with opals shaped like the moonflower which is your emblem - your dress is made completely of some golden material, again decorated with the flower opals. Before you is a great milky white carpet of the real flowers which the kneeling people before you have strewn at your feet. Your golden braids are entwined with the same flowers and an opal circlet rests on your head. A beautiful young man with deep dark eyes and a passionate light in their depths, eyes which mirror the fulfilment of that future passion, gaze at you with adoration as you gaze back at the beloved one as he slips this very same ring on your finger as a sign that you are betrothed to him... now the image is distorted, great waves crash on a rocky shore and the man of dark beauty holds your head above the water and kisses your salt wet lips with a desperate passion as if to make the kiss last for eternity... then he whispers... "remember my darling, I will love you - always!" and then the wave closes over your heads..." here the woman opened her eyes, gave a slight shake and gave the ring back.

Lunaflora, hypnotized by what the woman was saying had a sudden vision or memory. She was walking hand in hand with her lover and the scent of violets which grew six feet tall in that exotic green paradise came across in great overpowering waves, as if their perfume was the very essence and power of love itself!

Always a Romance of Lemuria

Still somewhat disturbed by what the clairvoyant had told her, when Lunaflora arrived home that evening she ran a video of one of Tristan's old films, films sometimes difficult to buy, though strangely some were being released, otherwise it meant recording them at the rare times they were on TV.

The film was not the one with the other Lunaflora, it was one he had made three or four years before they met - it was one of the few musicals he had made, it was one of Lunaflora's favourites. It was actually a biopic – 'The Marco de Vega Story', the story of a real life popular and brilliant pianist who was a near contemporary of Tristan - in fact they had known each other slightly - it strangely shadowed Tristan's own life.

In the film he depicted a much younger man at the beginning, how he worked his way up from nightclubs, became famous, he had been something like Tristan, dark and with a flashing smile which made the ladies swoon! Tristan could not play the piano but he made a good job of appearing to do so, with the actual music of the real pianist who fortunately had left many recordings. The pianist had married a society beauty, they had been very much in love, the sensuality behind Tristan's reserve broke through in this picture as he depicted the musician with his new bride - played by a blonde starlet who became a well known actress - then the tragedy when his wife died in childbirth, his rejection of their daughter, his delight in finding his daughter had inherited his gift for piano, then tragedy again when he discovered he was dying of a heart condition, just after finding love again with his young secretary - then the end of the film where he has a new wife and he has to tell his daughter that he is dying.

"Just when everything goes well, it's taken away from you," he says and then the fade out - as he and his daughter play his signature tune together - 'Liebestraum' by Liszt – it always produced tears - but his music lived on through his daughter who is playing piano alone in the last shot!

It was strange, thought Lunaflora, how the life of the subject of the film almost paralleled that of the actor playing him - were these things coincidences or were they shadows or perhaps sometimes warnings of things that were to be - but in some cases could yet be avoided? This was one of those eternal questions as unanswerable as the mysterious dreams and visions of Lunaflora and the clairvoyant she had seen only that afternoon!

After Lunaflora had finished watching the film, suddenly the inspiration for one of her rare poems came into her mind and about one hour later it was finished. She read it through, making minor adjustments, and then read it aloud:

"In dreams I wander with you,
Through starry skies of time,
Through realms where we never met,
Though we love forever.
I reach out for you,
Your dark drugging beauty
Crushes me to you,
Body and Soul -
My soul drowns in the fathomless depths of your passionate eyes,
And makes my bodily senses reel
With desire filled ecstasy,
As that beautiful mouth crashes against mine,
Like a violent hungry sea,
Crashes against golden parched sand -
Yearning beneath the sun,
For your thundering tidal wave
Of drowned fulfilment,
And the aftermath of screaming joy,
That is love's desire,
Fulfilled at last,
Yet forever - with you -
Just a Dream!

Chapter Three

Lunaflora had arrived in Hollywood - she couldn't yet believe it! It's funny when you're suddenly in a place you've only dreamed, read about, or seen on the screen, and then when you're suddenly there - for real - you do feel as if you must still be dreaming; it takes a while to sink in! But there in the distance were those famous giant sized letters on the hillside – HOLLYWOOD - it must be true! Yet her eyes were not really focused on those letters, exciting as they were - they were focused on her inner vision of a man's face - the face of Tristan Zennor - who seemed closer in this place, after all a part of him lay in a particular place and the knowledge that she would see this place the following day made her heart lurch with a mixture of grief, pain, yet strangely a kind of joyful ecstasy!

What had that clairvoyant said, 'he was, is and will be with you always'. Strange that 'Always' was the name of the book which had started it all. She seemed to recall words from somewhere else that echoed what she had experienced, whether they came from a book or film she could not recall, but they floated into her mind – 'I know now that nothing is a coincidence that every minute, every second of our time and existence is measured -

nothing is chance!' Was it true? Something told her it was, some sudden inner conviction from inside and yet outside herself, a sudden breeze stirred the curtains at the open window of the luxurious bedroom in the hotel suite she had been given, the dying but still bright Californian sunshine shafted like a golden path across the floor, the curtains lifted again in the breeze which caressed her face like the gentle hand of an invisible presence and for one glorious second she felt that presence, knew that beloved presence and a voice spoke in her heart as surely as if they had been spoken aloud, and that voice, wafted by the gentle breeze seemed to say with a kind of tenderness – 'This is not the end', and tomorrow she would visit his grave!

1955

Tristan Zennor paced impatiently up and down his bedroom at his mansion home 'Sea Breeze' which overlooked the Pacific Ocean. He'd been able to keep this house from being grabbed by both of his ex wives, well - almost his ex wife in the case of Conchita. He'd designed the house himself, a man of many talents; he thought grimly, perhaps too many talents.

He caught sight of himself in the full length mirrors on the beautiful grey and silver wardrobes. Such excellent taste people said, of his interior decoration. The mirror showed the face and figure of the man they called 'the most handsome man in the world', and completely without vanity for a moment he studied himself. The slim but muscular figure in an open necked shirt and light coloured trousers, the unconscious grace of his every movement, the well shaped elegant, yet strong hands that had wielded a sword so often and helped to do his own stunts. But above all the face that millions of women the world over screamed and fainted over! Wide, well shaped mouth, high cheek bones, high forehead, thick, slightly wavy black hair slicked back in the style of the day, and most of all those wonderful black luminous eyes, thickly lashed under shapely eyebrows!

Those eyes which could speak almost by themselves, but with the addition of that beautifully modulated, low, but clear, and very very seductive voice that could hold an audience and certainly any woman he wanted completely spellbound... as if they were under an enchantment... for always... he said to his reflection.

He turned away from his reflection and picked up his gold cigarette case, a present from Lunaflora, she had given him this the night he had given her the ring of opals shaped like a moonflower. He had come across it in a tucked away antique shop in a narrow street in the old part of San Francisco. It was almost uncanny how he'd spotted it in the window, it was exactly like the one described in the book 'Always' which Lunaflora had

Always a Romance of Lemuria

introduced to him a year or so ago when they had first met in England, and which now was being made into a screenplay for his new film, and which the producer and director at the studio were arguing over on this rather dull January day!

Lovely though the story in itself was, it was more the ideas in the book which fascinated him, past lives - it was almost as if he knew the story, as if he'd been part of it, the very character he was to play, he'd even dreamed about it, and his beautiful Moonflower/Lunaflora was there too... in those dreams. The main hitch to the production of the film was that Jean Marshall had pulled out... to become a housewife.... he smiled grimly... he wondered how long that would last! In any case it suited him, he wanted Lunaflora to play the part, it was made for her. He'd got her into the picture as an extra, after bringing her with him from England, and now he was going to make her a star... at least of this film... but mainly of his heart. She'd had a screen test and the powers that be at Romulus had been very enthusiastic and had signed her. It was now a case of deciding when and where they were going to start the picture.

Slowly, he opened the gold cigarette case and started to draw out a cigarette, even in that trivial action, with an unconscious grace, he hesitated, a tender smile curving the well shaped mouth and lighting up those wonderful eyes. There was an inscription inside the lid - just one word 'Toujours' – 'Always', Lunaflora's idea, and the same word was inscribed around the band of her moonflower ring. They had chosen French, His mother had been a French stage actress, Violette Dubois, she had met his father when they were appearing together in London and soon after had gone to America on tour where they were married and Tristan and his two sisters had come along.

Tristan was bi-lingual, brought up to speak French and English equally well, and at college had studied Italian and Spanish in addition to dramatic art. It was from his mother that he also got his exotic dark beauty, only his nose was a little like his father's, although he too had been a handsome man. As he lit his cigarette with the matching gold lighter, his gaze came to rest on his present wife Conchita Perez.

He had met Conchita Perez when he had been filming 'For Isabella and Spain', one of his better costume roles, with plenty of the action and swordsmanship he was famous for. He played the rather unlikely part of a Spanish nobleman turned soldier, fictional of course, with whom the fifteenth century Spanish queen Isabella was supposed to have fallen in love with, but naturally had to sacrifice him to marry the future Emperor Charles V, exit nobleman, but it had been a good part, telling the story of those troubled times based on a successful historical novel.

Conchita had played the part of a lady in waiting, 'literally' thought Tristan with a slight smile. For at the time he had just broken with a famous blonde actress whom he had been planning to marry. It didn't happen for one reason or another. The decision was his - he wasn't intentionally cruel, but so many of the women in his life wanted not so much as to love as to merely possess! So, one more broken heart, well, he was famous for it, and the exotic, dark, entirely different Conchita had replaced her. Perhaps at the time he had imagined himself in love with her, he was good at that too, deceiving even himself, and he had married her. He soon found out what a big mistake he had made. In spite of being married to the one of the most sought after and handsome men in the world, she just wasn't satisfied, any presentable actor, or in the case of a producer or director, they didn't even have to be presentable as long as they might be good for her own career! She wasn't interested in family life; she told him that she didn't want any children! Marta, his first wife, she had been a good wife too, he reflected sadly, it was just that he couldn't stay away from other women, so she had divorced him! Poor Marta wanted children, but couldn't have any. Now he was on the receiving end! Conchita, the year before had struck lucky and landed the leading female role of the character of the woman who had been the real 'Mona Lisa', in true Hollywood style in a musical biopic of the painter called 'The Great Leonardo'. The title role was being played by a gifted American-Italian tenor this particular big studio had recently discovered called Angelo Baretta!

Tristan laughed aloud - that fellow Leonardo really was a genius, he could paint, design aeroplanes hundreds of years before they were invented and SING! That was Hollywood for you!

Nevertheless, Tristan had great admiration for the owner of this incredible singing voice, and it was turning out to be a good film, many said it would make the new tenor's career and make the movie moguls very happy financially! Yes this Angelo was a great singer, a typical handsome Latin type, and unfortunately a typically great Latin lover - and the latest conquest was Conchita! Ironically the singer was a happily married family man and his wife knew about his womanizing and simply didn't seem to care. Tristan had met him at a party, he was a nice, likeable, if temperamental young man and under different circumstances they could have been friends. But he had provided the excuse Tristan wanted to divorce Conchita, especially now!

He picked up the framed photograph of Conchita with her whiter than white teeth, which did not entirely owe their even shape and whiteness to nature - in fact the extensive dental work on them had been paid for by the most famous of Tristan's former actor friends! This star, had briefly been Conchita's lover before she met Tristan, and the same star, wrote in his unvarnished memoirs years later 'and she still owes me the money for her dental work!' He also said, for years before, his boozing womanizing circle had included Tristan, and unlike some of the other male stars, he was not jealous of male rivals, not even Tristan who could lose even him for looks and attracting women, even he said in his book –'Tristan Zennor was a dope to marry Conchita!'

Tristan was never to know about that remark as he put the photo in a desk drawer, snapping it shut with both relief and disgust at her but also at himself, then he did something that would have horrified his studio and certainly his fans! All the tension, despair and worry, amounting to grief, welled up in him and he threw down the cigarette, sat on the bed, held his face in his hands and sobbed, as he had not sobbed since the death of his mother five years ago, this, if his fans could see him, was the real Tristan - all the trappings of a star, and sophisticated witty ladies' man stripped away, what he might have been, might yet be if the fates were kind - not only a true gentleman, but a man of great sensitivity and imagination that was the hallmark of the true artist, a sensitivity that made him feel aware of all the beauty of the world - and most of all - of the pain and suffering of the world - of every living thing, but even without an artistic bent, he would have been an extraordinarily kind person, one who hated to hurt people's feelings, not that he couldn't be angry and tough if need be, his war record was a tribute to that part of him, he'd been decorated, but his generosity and kindness, the ability to make friends, was rare indeed in a place like Hollywood. He was among the first group of actors in films to start a campaign to put an end to the callous use of horses and other animals, in motion pictures, which did indeed lead to a greater amount of care and kindness where animals were necessary.

Unfortunately like other true artists, the gift of feeling the pain of others meant that he experienced greater suffering in himself though not necessarily for himself than the average person, which was the price that gifted people have to pay. He despised the hard boiled cynical sophistication that his friends and colleagues displayed, men and women alike, and that he had to pretend to display himself, in some ways he was only his true self when he was acting, only really alive when he was acting! It was only then that the luminous sensitivity he possessed projected itself through those glorious eyes, the camera giving him close ups that no other male star had ever been given - mystifying and annoying his leading ladies when he first became a star twenty years before - until they were too drugged by his looks and seductive charm to care who got the best shots! That was when his main problem started... women... no one who had known the beautiful but shy and modest youth, earnestly working backstage and on stage in small parts in pre-Hollywood days would have dreamed of his future reputation for more affairs with attractive actresses than any other star in Hollywood! Although it was true he enjoyed flirting, it wasn't so much that he always chased and seduced women... it was the women who seduced him and did most of the chasing... and as long as they were attractive... he didn't put up much resistance. The only excuse he could offer, was that like the great poet Robert Burns, another hopeless romantic, quite often he genuinely imagined he was in love with them. For as his closest sister said to him; "you are simply chasing the shadow of real love to find the true substance of real love". She was right. He knew deep down, that he wasn't a cheap womaniser like most of the others – so why did he do it? He didn't know. When he met Marta he thought he had found the substance... for a time, she had all the right qualities, beauty, high intelligence, culture, a love of beauty, books, music, poetry.

They had met when he had begun work on one of his best early roles, in the film 'Phoenix', a typical Hollywood style saga of an otherwise excellent film of the late thirties, in which he played 'Sir Christopher Wren' and the building of his great cathedral 'St Paul's', Marta Helman had been the historically imaginary German princess with whom he fell in love and who had to be killed off in the Great Fire of London, so he could pursue his architectural dreams and naturally true stuff of Hollywood romance her ghost stood beside him as he gazed on the wonderful building that was the realisation of his dream!

Marta, a successful star in her own country, had been chosen for the part and they did fall in love and were married, he tried, but back came 'the other women'.

"Why did you do it? I know in my heart... it's not the REAL YOU!" Marta had said the day she left, "it's not your true nature to be promiscuous like all the others," he couldn't answer, he didn't know, it was perhaps just as well they had no children. It was almost as if... in every pretty face he saw... he was looking for a particular face... he didn't even know what she looked like... yet he knew he would recognise her when he saw her. It was about this time that he started having those dreams... he was in the dreams... and there was a girl... he somehow knew that this was the girl he was searching for... his true love... it seemed as if he had always known her. In one dream they were embracing in a great marble hall, heavy with the scent of flowers that he knew to be moonflowers but many times larger than they were in this world, but as often happens in dreams, he never saw the girl's face, even though he knew her. The dreams didn't occur often, at least not until around the time Marta had left him and Jenny had stepped into his life with an old book called 'Always'.

Chapter Four

Jenny Rainer was a top musical star before Tristan Zennor began his film career. He had had a crush on her when as a youth of eighteen or so he saw her on the screen in her most memorable role in 'Shooting Star', he didn't dream then that only a few years later he would be meeting her at a party after his first starring role in 'The Rothschild's' of Paris', the story of the great banking family at the end of the 18th century.

After this film's release he was literally a star overnight - success had come quickly, perhaps too quickly, he'd hardly had any small parts to start with... no apprenticeship for this bright young man - the studio knew what they had discovered - a born actor of physical beauty that was a gift to the camera and to their profits! He was mobbed by thousands of screaming girls and women, and unlike many stars, he could handle it, he never minded how many autographs he signed, never grew impatient, and it would be those very qualities that would also endear him to posterity. He wasted no time in making the acquaintance of Jenny Rainer. Though eight years his senior, she was tiny, with curly auburn hair and large brown eyes and looked much younger. She was at first flattered at the obvious adulation of her by this handsome, still boyish young man. She had just been divorced from a business man who had strange preferences. She and Tristan became friends, she was known as 'the Cutie with the IQ', she may have started out as a chorus girl but she had majored in philosophy at college. Tristan liked intelligent as well as attractive women, but their friendship didn't become more than friendship until his separation from Marta Helman.

His sisters were to say, years later, that apart from the girl he died with, they and their mother had liked Jenny Rainer the best, they always hoped he would marry her! It was certainly a great love affair! Tristan remembered the evening when, in another part of this very house, in his 'playroom' as Marta had jokingly called it, where he kept all his books and records and a few paintings, not perhaps by famous artists, but ones he liked, a place above all where he could relax, and at that point in time relax with whoever he liked!

Jenny had introduced Tristan to Polynesian music, particularly Hawaiian music and they were sitting close together before the open fire, listening to some of those records. It was a cold December evening, but was warm in the room, and if he closed his eyes, almost half asleep, the warmth was not a fire, but the warmth of a tropical sun as the surf raced in beneath the palm trees, over the gold-white sand. It was almost as if it was a memory, the melodies seemed familiar, and there seemed to be a beautiful girl singing, singing of their love and calling to him, his Moonflower standing not so far from that golden beach amidst the crystal waterfalls cascading down like her beautiful hair in the midst of the snow white blossoms in the Valley of the Moonflowers!

It was at that point that the record ended, he jumped up to stop the gramophone, and still slightly dazed from his dream, he gazed at Jenny as if she was a stranger, she didn't seem to notice but merely placed an old book in his hands as he sat down again. He looked at the title, it was called 'Always'.

"I think you'll like this book'" Jenny said, "'it was my mother's, she read it just before I was born, she got me interested in the ideas in it, who knows, maybe it could be a film, it's certainly made for you, maybe for me as well."

She leaned back on the sofa at the look in his eyes, that look that turned probably millions of women to water, as his lips descended on hers, and yet had she known it, as his lips met hers with a ravenous, passionate desire, it was not Jenny Rainer he was kissing but a blue eyed girl with moonflowers in her golden hair!

PRESENT

The next morning, Lunaflora found herself standing by the grave of the man she had loved all her life, and which was also the grave of the woman who had looked so like herself. It was surrounded by smooth lawns near other graves and monuments to stars that had talked and laughed with Tristan Zennor, some even who had appeared on screen with him.

At the feet of the angel which guarded the grave with outstretched wings, a pristine white female looking angel with long flowing hair frozen in time and stone, clumps of California poppies as yellow as the sun in which they shone, not red like most English ones, but like the petals of the ballet tutu that the divine Anna Pavlova had worn for her famous solo – 'California Poppy' which Lunaflora knew Tristan, as a child, had seen the great ballerina dance on one of her American tours. Lunaflora looked at the simple inscription, just the date of Tristan's birth and death, his occupation, and in smaller lettering details of the woman he died with – finally 'Omnia vincit amor' – Love Conquers All! Lunaflora guessed that it was his two sisters and first wife who had seen that these two were buried together and the inscription, his second wife would not have been so generous. Lunaflora seemed to vaguely remember that his divorce from his second wife – one of those quick Mexican divorces – had been final some time before this tragedy. She knew that one of his sisters was still alive – Demelza Zennor Ravenna, the only one of the three who had had any children, a son and a daughter, the son named after his uncle – Tristan Zennor Ravenna, his father having been an Italian. The nephew was not an actor, but an opera singer – more Lunaflora did not know, in any case he lived in Italy, but he didn't seem to be known outside that country. Did he resemble his beautiful uncle thought the girl musingly. She didn't know that either. Probably not, there could never be two like that, even if there was a resemblance. The only certain thing was that his mother, Demelza, the favourite sister had given birth to this son prematurely, just two weeks later, after and because of the shock of her brother's death!

She knelt down and after kissing the blood red petals of the nearest flower, placed the spray of deep red roses on the grave, and as she did so a sudden wind blew up and the stone face of the angel which she only just realized was her mirror image, and no doubt that of the woman who lay buried there, the lowered eyes of the angel seemed to look directly at Lunaflora and the stone lips widened into a smile at once mysterious yet full of a kind of compassion and hope. The smile and the sun seemed to get brighter and the wind whirled it into a dizzying merry-go-round... round and round... and there

Always a Romance of Lemuria

was a humming both inside and outside of Lunaflora... like the hum of time itself... and she was whirled into a whirlwind which went backwards and catapulted her into a dark tunnel like the ghost train opposite the merry-go-round until there was only a feeling of being carried and yet at the same time lulled into a soft blue blanket of the darkest midnight blue overlaid with the sweetness of pink candyfloss and the soft pink fur of her childhood teddy bear into the sweetness of complete oblivion!

Chapter Five

1955

Lunaflora awoke, no longer standing by a grave but in what appeared to be a hospital room, a private room - transformed into a garden of vases overflowing with mainly roses, red, white, yellow, and masses of marguerites - like moonflowers, she thought. In the centre of the 'garden' was a white hospital bed, in the bed lay a girl - the other Lunaflora - like a Sleeping Beauty yet whose skin was as pale as Snow White. She was dressed in a flimsy blue nightdress, a bed jacket over it, and her gold blonde hair was braided and tied with a blue ribbon.

Am I dreaming thought the modern Lunaflora the blue woollen dress she wore with its full skirt seemed real enough, she pinched her own arm, "ah, that certainly hurt", well they say be careful what you wish for, it might come true - had she been transported to a time before she was born? She saw a large calendar on the wall - January 1955! - had the girl been ill? She drew close to the bed, then realised that she herself, in the light from the window, cast no shadow, her feet made no sound on the polished floor, she was a ghost from the future!

She leaned over the girl in the bed, there was no fall and rise of breathing evident, no movement, gingerly she put her hand over the girl's heart... no heartbeat... she jumped back in horror... the girl in the bed was dead! She then noticed a dressing on the girl's temple - some kind of accident perhaps!

Suddenly the door opened, a doctor in a white coat entered, with a nurse in the old fashioned all white American nurse's uniform. Lunaflora jumped back, forgetting they couldn't see her. The doctor leaned over the girl in the bed, felt her pulse, used his stethoscope. He glanced up at the drip and other things attached to the girl's arm.

"'That won't be necessary any longer nurse". The nurse's head snapped up.

"'You mean...?'"

"'I'm afraid this lovely girl is no longer merely comatose, she's dead." The nurse turned as pale as the deceased patient.

"'But surely it was just very severe concussion!'" ''There must have been some complication - she fell and hit her head - possibly there was haemorrhaging - these things happen, she was comatose, but we thought it was temporary, I did not actually see her myself when she was admitted, there may have been a bad fracture, we all know that particular doctor's reputation, who initially examined her, even X-rays can be faulty sometimes."

"There'll be a post mortem," said the nurse. The doctor shook his head.

"'New to Hollywood aren't you my dear! There will be no post mortem, the girl's studio and her world famous boyfriend will see to that - even if they suspect neglect and don't you think the hospital will co-operate... the press would have a field day... 'Hollywood hospital neglect causes death of beautiful young star and fiancée of the world's leading male screen idol' - no Nurse Reagan - her cause of death will be unfortunate brain haemorrhage caused by accident... come on... let's face the Hollywood music and get it over with." They left behind a dead girl and her ghostly double. The ghost looked at her former dead physical self in a kind of bewildered horror and suddenly she felt her own body floating high above the bed - she saw the body in the bed slowly fading away until it disappeared completely and she felt her own body, intact with its spirit descending to the bed until there was a blackness and she knew no more!

After what seemed to be a long, long time, she came around to find herself lying in the bed, and raising herself slightly, to her astonishment she found that she was wearing what appeared to be the same clothes as her deceased double. It gave her a slight shiver, then it suddenly hit her that whatever intelligence had put her back in time and in the other girl's place - from now on... though she was the Lunaflora from 1990 – herself... and not some former self... from now on she had to pretend to be the other Lunaflora who had just died... and so would have to use her own ability as an actress... and the first hurdle was to act the part of an apparently dead girl who had just come back to life... and the next few seconds would count... because with a heart beating so loudly that she thought she might really die... she heard the footsteps approaching her room, footsteps that she knew as well as her own... but ones that she had only heard in old films and in her wildest dreams!

Lunaflora lay back on the pillows, imitating the dead girl she had replaced - except that SHE was alive! Through her eyelashes she saw the door slowly open, and framed in the doorway, with her heart beating as if it would beat its way out of her body - stood a man - time stood still - maybe literally - for there stood Tristan Zennor, casually dressed, a bouquet of red roses in one hand and a large oblong box under his arm, those glorious eyes unashamedly weeping - and with the tears of decades and untold ages cascading from her own eyes, the girl from the future and the past sat up in bed and stretched out her arms to the man she adored - calling his name - and time ceased to exist - as he dropped the flowers and the box and in two strides held her in his arms, kissing her with those lips that she had only dreamed of or imagined, and he clasped her to his body so tight that her breath seemed to stop and she clung tightly to him so much that it was a kind of death and rebirth in one moment of eternity that had been eternity from the beginning of time and would have no end but was forever and always!

After what seemed several lifetimes, he placed her gently back against the pillows, and with a melody rushing through her senses and whirling head that she knew from one of his films - he said:

"'My beloved... they said you were dead... they must have been mistaken". She raised her hand wonderingly to his hair... and answered "if you love someone enough... anything can happen...even miracles... beloved!"

Tristan took a deep breath, and tried to gather his emotions, "'I'd better go and have a word with the doctor, otherwise he may die of shock!" he said with an attempt at lightness.

"In the meantime, my darling, here is something to amuse you." He picked up the bouquet of red roses and put them on a table beside the bed.

"Oh, how lovely," whispered Lunaflora but it was the very large oblong box that he placed in her arms. He removed the lid and the layers of scented tissue papery framed in the box was a three foot high plus... doll... a doll with a body made of soft brown velvet, a Hawaiian doll with glossy black hair which hung to her waist, large black eyes and smiling red lips, a grass skirt and matching top, long brown legs and bare feet with ankle bracelets of flowers. A white garland adorned her head - but around her neck not the single white flower lei of the doll but a real multi strand waist length white lei made of the most expensive kind of Hawaiian Ni-hau shell, wound twice around the doll's neck. Tristan removed the shell lei and hung it around Lunaflora's neck, where if she was upright it would have hung to her waist - the cost of it could only be guessed!

"Oh Tristan, it's wonderful!" He pulled her gently to him and once more kissed her before he went to fetch the doctor.

The new Lunaflora, still reeling with shock realized that the other girl must have shared her own love of collecting beautiful dolls, beautiful jewels, and sometimes unusual stuffed toys... Tristan had obviously indulged the 'other girl' and nothing was too good or too expensive! Never had Lunaflora possessed any necklace so exotic, and she knew in her own 1990 terms that such a piece of jewellery would cost thousands of dollars, still perhaps in the time she was in and her own time it was a fairly moderate purchase for a world famous movie star!

Quick footsteps sounded in the corridor, she dug her nails into the palms of her hands in a panic, her mouth was dry... would the doctor know she was a different person? Or at least a different 'body'. Then she relaxed, even if he suspected something different about her, he would not believe her even if she told him, he would think she was mad.

The doctor followed Tristan into the room and went off balance slightly with almost the same shock as Tristan. He went to her, felt her pulse, put his stethoscope to her chest, looked in her eyes, then stood back.

"Well, young woman, I don't know what has happened here, miracles have been known to happen and this must be one of them... there is no other explanation". Lunaflora picked up the doll and clutched it like a child with a secret, glanced at the man she loved and thought... "if only they knew!"

Chapter Six

The next day Lunaflora was allowed out of hospital after a final check up by the amazed staff. She was placed very carefully in the back of Tristan's limousine together with the flowers, the doll, and the clothes that had belonged to the other girl.

She still felt rather dazed though endeavouring to keep up the part she was playing. Tristan could not do enough for her. He didn't use the limousine very often, it was just part of the Hollywood paraphernalia. He preferred his Cadillac, which was a discreet cream colour, but for his favourite patients, the limousine was the thing!

"Where are we going?" Lunaflora asked him, as she was put into the car.

"Well, not back to your hotel," he said, "I think under the circumstances you'd better come home with me." She looked at him a little startled, she thought quickly.

"I - I can't seem to remember much, in fact I can't remember anything at all of what happened to me." Tristan looked at her very hard.

"The doctor did say that there was a possibility that your short term memory could be affected," he said, "I'll have to remind you of things... and things,'" he went on with one of those meaningful smiles that made her head really spin and heat sweep through her body, and her face burned as his eyes lingered on her, then he gave that low seductive laugh and got into the front passenger seat beside the chauffeur!

The only thing she could see on the way to the destination, for although January, there was a bright blue sky, the tops of palm trees, the occasional roof and in the busy streets they went through, a few curious eyes. Then they were beyond the outskirts of the city and seemed to be on a rather bumpy road.

All she could now see were the tops of stark yellowish coloured rocks against even more blue sky. She thought she could detect the salt laden smell of the sea as they neared the coast and Tristan's home. She saw seagulls wheeling across the blue and their faint cry, exactly the same cry as she heard in her native English West Country, almost as if she expected the Californian seagulls to have a different sound she thought with slight amusement... as if they should be speaking a foreign language or have an American accent! All these rather silly thoughts ran through her mind in the shock and upside down feeling of being in another time and another world. The car carried on in silence then Tristan turned around in his seat and looked at Lunaflora with a tender look in his eyes.

"Well, my sleeping beauty," he said softly, "we're nearly home." Lunaflora raised herself on one elbow, then a little more until she was almost sitting and she found that they were going down a hill and ahead of them was the endless blue green expanse of the Pacific Ocean and on a rocky headland, a little to the right and with what appeared to be a beautiful garden all around, was a slightly Spanish style house almost hidden by beautiful trees like a protective circle around it.

"'Oh - how beautiful!'" she whispered. Tristan looked at her a little curiously.

"'That accident must have affected your memory quite badly,'" he said slowly, you've been here several times... more than several."

"Well," she answered, "I just don't seem to remember anything."

"'Well... you will!" he said, and they lapsed into silence, while Lunaflora continued to look at that expanse of ocean, and somewhere in her mind she seemed to see land where there was now water, great trees, mighty buildings, like pyramids, soaring towers where there was now just blue green ocean, and this land they were now on seemed somehow to have been part of it, but it was all just a jumble in her mind. She seemed to know that once, long ago, in another lifetime, the land did not end here but went straight on to the seemingly endless horizon.

Always a Romance of Lemuria

During the few miles that remained on the way to the house, Lunaflora drifted off into quite a deep sleep, she was only vaguely conscious of strong arms carrying her from the car into a building. She was too drowsy even to open her eyes, although she was... even in that state excitedly aware of who was carrying her. They went up a steep flight of stairs, she felt herself being carried through a door and deposited on a bed which was when she opened her eyes, and the first thing she noticed was that she was lying on a tester bed, and the curtains and bed hangings were of a soft pale green, beautifully embroidered with white moonflowers just like those she'd seen in her dreams!

On the floor, the little she could see of it, was a soft green carpet and the walls were one gigantic tapestry, a scene of waving palm trees intertwined with the same motif of enormous white Moonflowers. As she opened her eyes fully, she saw those fantastically beautiful eyes gazing down at her, full of tender concern, and her heart leapt to meet them! There was also a strange look of peace in their deep dark blackness, mixed with a love that her soul would have willingly drowned itself in!

"I'll leave you to rest,'" he said gently, "and later on I'll have some refreshment sent up to you," and with that he half lifted her into his arms and gave her a kiss of such passion, which she returned and seemed to drain all the life from her willingly... and even her spirit. He laid her back against the pillows, silently left the room and she drifted into sleep.

The next time she awoke, she half sat up and glanced at a small clock on the ornate bedside table, it said 1:30, so it was early afternoon. She still felt dazed. She looked around the room. She noticed that at one end, near what looked like an antique French writing desk, there was a kind of large alcove, lined with shelves. On the lower shelves were a lot of books, but on the shelves above, as she had suspected there would be, was a collection of wonderful dolls, some in foreign costume, some just beautiful in themselves, and there were also some unusual soft toys. They were very much like the ones she had in her own home, in her own time. Sitting in the chair in front of the writing desk was the latest addition, the largest doll, the Hawaiian doll with a mysterious little smile on her brown velvet face!

The door suddenly opened and Tristan walked in carrying a tray.

"I've brought you something to eat,'" he said, "it's your favourite light meal." She sat up against the pillows and placed the tray across her knees. The light meal consisted of French bread and butter, a dish on which there was a substantial amount of cottage cheese and a

Always a Romance of Lemuria

plate with a beautiful bunch of blue black grapes on it and a tall glass of fresh orange juice.

"Thank you," she said, a little shyly. She still had not got used to the fact that the man she had only dreamed about was right by her side. He bent down and kissed her and then said:

"I'll leave you in peace to eat it, I'll be back later," and with one of those smiles that seemed to stay and light up the room long after he was gone, he went out, closing the door softly behind him.

She quickly ate the contents of the tray, in spite of her bemusement, she was hungry, and what was on the tray was certainly delicious! After she had finished she placed the tray on the floor at the side of the bed. She felt suddenly very tired and she quickly drifted into a deep but strangely peaceful slumber.

Lunaflora opened her eyes and awoke - or was she dreaming? She sat up in sudden fear. Was she still back there with her lover in 1955 or was she in the hotel of 1990? No... she was still in that room that was today yet yesterday. She looked through the window which overlooked a terrace and the now molten gold of the endless Pacific Ocean as the sun sank low, a glowing rose of fire and ruby red gold sending out shooting golden streamers through her window mingling with the lengthening shadows in the room. A cool breeze blew in also and she shivered in the flimsy negligee... so flimsy she suddenly realized that her cheeks burned like the red rose fire of the Californian sunset. When she thought of him her head and heart thumped so hard that she swayed back against the pillows! Was it possible to be delirious with excitement and raw passion yet feel a peace she had never felt in her life except... as it were... 'through a glass darkly' when she looked into those wonderful eyes... but on a screen in her own time of a person who there, was long dead, but was now alive in his own time... his reality... where he was alive and she knew in that short time that he felt the same as she did.

Yet he thought she was that other girl... and was she the same girl born again into her own time and existence? The answer must be an unexplainable yes - so why was he not there in her own time... in the form of someone else? There was no answer, only the timeless silence and the gigantic stars which had begun to shine, lighted by a Deity in which she steadfastly believed, and she repeated the line from an old film where past and present mingled for the sake of a great love and which almost mirrored her own tremendous experience...

"God knows," she said aloud, repeating the well remembered line, and as if he knew the same film and line, that beloved voice from the doorway answered – "I think he does Lunaflora".

Lunaflora saw Tristan in a dark dinner jacket... that and the pristine whiteness of his shirt highlighting afresh for her the incredible beauty of this man framed in the doorway.

He looked both apologetic and disappointed as his gaze swept her blue ribboned flowing hair and the quick rise and fall of her very full breasts on which his passionate eyes lingered for an endless moment of time and which produced images in her mind that made her face burn very brightly indeed and she suddenly felt very hot, evidence which did not escape his hypnotic gaze as he replied with that seductive, half amused look that had made millions of women swoon, he said:

"Duty calls dearest, dinner with the Director and the powers that be I'm afraid, but just ring if you want anything... until tonight then...'" he whispered in a way that made her heart turn somersaults, and with a great reluctance, he turned on his heel and she heard his quick footsteps running down the staircase... as if he had to leave before... and her blood pounded with the possibilities she had never realized might actually come true! She turned her head and in the still light room she saw a photograph of Tristan in his most famous and one of the few dramatic roles that he had used his great gifts, it was a still from 'The Eye of a Needle', taken from the novel by a famous English novelist, about a man who was searching for the meaning of life after the horrors of war, the photo was the still where his search for truth is to some degree answered, a beautiful close up at the sacred high point of the film, the one film for which he won an academy award.

The room was getting dark, she could no longer see the objects clearly, moonlight shafted in through the window, she didn't bother to try and find out where the light was, although she thought there was a bedside lamp. The moonlight was enough and besides that she felt very tired after all she had come a long way, from another world. She once more leaned back against the pillows, fell asleep and this time dreamed.

In that dream, she was once again back in that far older world, a world before time, countless thousands of years before the twentieth century AD, a world where she and Tristan must have lived in another lifetime where they were together. In this dream she was a child again, of perhaps twelve, going into adolescence, but on the brink of womanhood.

Although conscious that she was dreaming, she was at once the person she had been, and yet the person she was now and that part of her was amazed at the things she saw in that dream. Again she was on that beautiful burning beach, white sand, palm trees, and other gigantic trees for which she had no name, she was laughing, throwing her head back and laughing as only a carefree child can, and she was riding on the back of the largest tortoise she had ever seen either in dreams or in life. Even the giant tortoises of the Galapagos Islands in her own time would seem very small in comparison to this one. It was roughly the size of a medium horse, and there she was, riding on its back, with a couple of girls, probably handmaidens running behind, somewhat out of breath, for, considering it was a tortoise it was moving pretty fast, and there were a few other tortoises of a similar size lumbering about nearby. In her arms, being the child she still was, was what appeared to be the very same doll that Tristan had just given her, although its dress was slightly different, in place of the grass skirt was one of gold thread, that shone dazzlingly under the burning sun, and around its neck, there were no shells, but a necklace of those beautiful opals shaped like moonflowers.

She herself, apart from her blonde colouring, was dressed almost identically to that of the doll, a skirt of gold thread that shimmered and danced as the tortoise lumbered along the beach. Around her top she wore a brief silk sash which did nothing to hide the roundness of her developing breasts , which already were those of a woman grown.

Riding towards her along the beach was the beautiful young man who was both Tristan and the young man of this other time, but unlike her clumsy and amusing steed, his steed, throwing up the silvery sands beneath its hooves was the most beautiful white horse Lunaflora had ever seen, again the animal was much larger than horses of her own time. Its back was draped with a material of red and gold. Astride the stallion, was the young man, dressed in a short bright red and blue tunic, golden sandals, fastened crisscross up his calves, showing his slim but muscular thighs, which even in the dream made the girl's blood race and her face burned with desire. His dark beauty was heightened by the golden helmet, from which sprang red and blue plumes, and the gold flashed under the burning sun as his beautiful white teeth flashed a smile at her as he drew near.

A pain shot through her body at the sight of him, yet, half child as she still was, she clutched the doll hard against her chest, suddenly shy, and realizing that the doll of the dream was not brown velvet but honey coloured wood. He noticed her action and noted the full beauty she tried to hide. She looked up for a moment to where he had come from, on a stone landing place some distance away, his crew busied themselves around what, to the modern girl's amazement appeared to be a huge flying machine, but so ornate that it was barely recognizable.

At the point she was studying the flying machine, a sudden rush of wind blew across her face - the dream ended and she was awake. She was back in her bedroom in Tristan's house and the wind was blowing through the window which had burst open. She slipped out of bed and closed the window, it might be California but it was January and the night was cold. The house was silent, though a light shone in the housekeeper and her gardener/chauffeur husband's quarters.

The bedside clock showed midnight... Tristan had not yet returned... her heart beat so hard at the thought of him that it almost seemed to choke her and she staggered against the half open door in the dark. She pulled the door open further and peered out. There was a dim light in the corridor... to her right was the landing and the grand staircase which led from the large square tiled hall below. This much she vaguely remembered. Another staircase led upwards to the second stored. Across from her room were two doors, but first she looked through the door next to her room. It was a bathroom... there was a sunken bath shaped like a white moonflower, the floor was of pale green tiles, the walls were white tiles with a motif of palm trees. There was a shower cubicle and a pale green wash basin fitted against a wall which was one huge mirror and fleecy white towels hung on rails, towels with 'Lunaflora' embroidered in one corner in green. Even the soap and various toiletries were of white or green. All this had been designed for the girl who she now replaced in preparation for the day she would come here as his wife!

What superb taste that amazing young man had! She pushed open another door which led into a small but adequate dressing room - which she realized led out of her bedroom. There was a beautiful dressing table, the kind with the... in this case... pale green frills which she had always admired... maybe fussy to some, but beautiful in her eyes. Silver backed hairbrush and comb, with a rare expensive perfume in a crystal bottle and every conceivable cosmetic. She pulled open a drawer... ribbons and hair ornaments, and in the drawer on the other side, a large jewel case of white velvet... and yes shaped like a moonflower and her name embroidered on it. She lifted the lid and laughed with delight, it was a musical jewel box and tinkled 'I'll be Loving You – Always'. Inside the box, not sparkling diamonds, just one necklace of opals, shaped like individual moonflowers, a matching bracelet, a matching large jewel flower for her hair, matching earrings, and in addition, a single strand of real pearls, plain gold loop earrings and a plain gold bangle... not for his future wife a pile of vulgar diamonds... and she felt a pang of envy for that other girl who had been herself and the other women who had shared his life, he knew what was best and he got the best... and in the best taste!

She put the jewel box back, closed the drawer and pulled back the sliding door of the fitted wardrobe, or as they would say – closet... and gazed... here the colours ran riot, all shades of the rainbow, blues of every hue from sky blue to turquoise, greens, pink and even reds, and one elegant black, and that was just the dresses. There were afternoon dresses, smart suits and the inevitable but beautiful hats, from berets to frothy concoctions, one for every outfit and there were also the most gorgeous matching shoes... and after a close inspection, Lunaflora realised that all these items, though made for... to some extent... another woman, might have made for herself, in fact they looked a perfect fit! She closed the door and wandered back into the dimly lit corridor and noticed another door that was slightly ajar opposite. She went in, felt for the light switch and flicked it on. She smiled and her eyes lit up at what she saw. It was a medium sized sitting room, a music room too. There was a small modern piano against one wall, she walked over to it, and looked at the music on the rest and again smiled - I'll be loving you Always – then the other girl must have played the piano as she herself could and probably sing. There was a pile of sheet music on top of the piano, a mixture of classical and popular music both vocal and for the piano... exactly the same music she had back in her own time on top of her own piano. There were two photographs in silver frames, one of Tristan, exactly the same one she had at home, and one of him and the other Lunaflora, his arm around her shoulder. Again Lunaflora felt a pang that could only be jealousy! She turned away and noticed that there was a television set inside a handsome cabinet in one corner, and she remembered half noticing a radiogram just inside the door, and suddenly a record began to play... a voice that had been silent in her world, except for his films and recordings, for the same length of time as darling Tristan... it was the wonderful, unforgettable voice of the great Mario Lanza singing 'Be My love' ... she whirled around with shock and a knife like pain of excitement and ecstasy pierced her heart because, by the radiogram, exquisite in evening clothes, and brilliant black eyes stood Tristan, holding out his arms towards her!

Chapter Seven

They looked at each other... Lunaflora was suddenly conscious of his immaculately groomed hair, so black, slightly waving, but not that blue black colour that was so popular in literature... but that other black - as now when the bright light from the standard lamp shone on it... his hair shone with the lustre of the darkest polished mahogany that contains the dark red glow of a dying flame, a flame which echoed itself in his eyes which made Lunaflora's body shudder from the jolt of her own heart as the light from her end of the room turned her flowing blonde hair to liquid golden honey, a honey, the sweetest of all, which was melting her body beneath his gaze as the last notes of Lanza's passionate voice soared between them, as if echoing the cry of their own hearts in the words 'be my love, for no-one else can end this yearning'!

Instinctively she ran into his outstretched arms and he lifted her from the floor and sank onto a nearby couch and bent his head until his beautiful mouth devoured her own parted hungry lips and those elegant hands explored her body in a way that made her blood thump to her head ready to explode at the long awaited outcome!... the vision of which had begun on a small flickering screen... in her past... yet when he no longer had a future!

Though this might have been the culmination of a dream that she had longed for all her life which until this 'time slip' which she could barely comprehend, though this fantasy had become a reality, some warning bell started to ring somewhere in her brain. She was being given a chance maybe no-one else had ever had in the entire history of the world, yet she knew it must not happen... not like this... and not yet!... much as her body and soul craved it. Why? She was not quite sure... partly though she was a young woman from the year 1990, and most people were pretty easy going with their morals, not even seeing any wrong in it... not everybody was the same... certainly not the modern Lunaflora... she wanted this not only with the man she loved but with the man she would marry and would have married... though never dreaming it would literally be the man of her dreams. Perhaps that other self that had died in that hospital had been through this, she wouldn't have blamed her, it was a strength she did not know she possessed to withdraw and give him a hard push, it almost broke her heart to do it, for his sake as much as her own. She expected anger and bewilderment... hurt... but when she raised her flushed face to meet his eyes, she saw to her amazement, only a kind of tender amusement mixed with resignation.

"'Aren't you angry?'" she asked in a harsh whisper.

"'No... you can't blame me for trying... and I know how much it cost you as well as myself to put an end to it. Perhaps we should blame it on the persuasive voice of Mr Lanza who I spoke to briefly at the party tonight." All at once Lunaflora forgot where she was... forgot it was 1955 for a moment she was mentally back in her own time and she blurted out...

"'That's impossible... Mario Lanza's been dead for thirty years!" There was an awful silence... as the awfulness of what she had just done hit her... 'blown her cover' if inadvertently... as the Americans would say. She put her hands over her face and started to cry with great shuddering sobs... so broken hearted that the hardest person would have been moved. The hands of the man she thought she'd betrayed and now lost forever gently pulled her hands away from her face... he tilted her chin gently until she was looking into those wonderful eyes through her tears... and he just said very gently and with that wonderful tenderness that so often had shone from his eyes and which did now...

"'Did you think, my heart's darling that didn't know, almost from the beginning... that I didn't guess... even though you deserve an Academy Award for best actress ever!.. he added, trying a joke to calm her down. She said nothing, she could not speak, so he just took her into his arms as he would a child, held her very close and rocked her until her sobs ceased... and until that kind of peace 'that passeth all understanding' was restored between them.

She looked up at last... her grey blue eyes enormous due to terror as well as tears... but saw only love in his eyes and her own reflection in their brilliant dark depths that had jolted her weary heart so many times on film.

"'How long have you known?'" she whispered. He drew her head down against his shoulder with his arms clasped tightly around her.

"I think unconsciously... from the moment I saw you in the hospital bed... consciously... during the journey home... you don't need to explain why... only perhaps how when you've calmed down more... I know in some mysterious way that though technically you are someone else... you don't just look like the other girl... YOU ARE the other girl who must have died in that hospital bed... you see even before I met... shall we say... You... Number One, I had curious dreams of not only you and I together in some long ago forgotten world... very like the world of this book and film 'Always', but since Jenny first gave me the book I also had dreams of you in yet a different world... my own world... but I think... somewhere in the future... a time I don't know. I've dreamed of you sitting in front of a kind of TV screen, typing on a weird kind of keyboard typing literary pieces which appear on the screen... and now and again you glance through a large window at a conical hill topped by a tower rising up from the mist... THAT... I recognised because I saw it in England just before I met the other you, you call it Glastonbury Tor, and your clothes, though very pretty, are quite different from the kind girls wear now, and there is always a large tabby cat by you, your doll collection, and a photo of me which you gaze at... the way you're gazing at me now!" Lunaflora's face burned at the way he was looking at her as he finished, and she wanted to look down but she held his gaze for only the truth would do.

"'What you say is true, the other girl or me, did die, at least physically in that hospital bed... and she told him how the other girl's body had disappeared and she had passed out to find herself in the other girl's place... in the bed where the doctor and nurse had discovered her.

"You see... you're right when you say I am from the future, I must be that girl born again... I was born in 1956... and when you see me in front of that screen it is the year 1990, that is my present,'" and she told him about her whole life up until that moment and her knowledge of the book 'Always', the film, and how she had always loved him since her childhood, how she had become a writer and had arrived in Hollywood for her own book to be made into a film.

Always a Romance of Lemuria

He took her out onto the balcony, how closer the stars were than in England... they seemed almost to be dipping into the ocean on the far horizon.

The music which had seemed to last for eternity died away and reluctantly leaving Lunaflora's side swiftly crossed the room and replaced the record... another of Lanza's, though one she was not familiar with... even for Lanza it was one of the most heart rendingly beautiful songs she had ever heard and Tristan returned and he thrust his hands into her golden hair and captured her mouth in a kiss of passion and violence that though making her senses reel, flooded her with desire and she forgot the shyness and slightly bewildering awe and pressed herself to him with a hunger that had waited a lifetime... perhaps a thousand lifetimes,... the title of the song spoke for itself... 'For You Alone'.

Tristan suddenly stopped himself and stepped back while Lunaflora stood with her eyes closed expectantly and then opened them in surprise and disappointment.

"No... my love... dearest one... the moment will come at the right time..." Tristan answered her silent question with the flame of promise in his eyes, and she dropped her own in confusion... "'but didn't that other me... she stuttered... didn't she and you....?"

"No... incredible as it may seem... we did not... she was a decent girl and we were planning to be married in secret... in fact it was to be the day after tomorrow... in a Spanish mission church near the shore, of course that was before your double fell down the slippery steps to the beach, when the studio was looking for possible film locations."

"Oh so that's what happened!" said Lunaflora.

"No problem now, you're fine my love and tomorrow my Mexican divorce is absolute - so Father Pedro will be waiting in the little chapel, the wedding music will be the music of the Pacific Ocean breaking on the beach below and you'll look beautiful in that cream silk dress, the opal clip in that beautiful long hair and a bouquet of red roses to rival those beautiful red lips and then" ...he crushed her to him until she felt her bones would break, returning his deep passionate kisses and pressing herself shamelessly as his hands moved sensuously upwards over her thudding rib cage and she moaned as they laid claim to her full breasts and a glorious feeling of heat and pleasurable pain gushed upwards like a red hot fountain from deep within her and his caresses increased as he became aware of her response and pressed the small of her back as she instinctively arched her body so that it fitted perfectly to him for the moment on the morrow when they would indeed be one at last!

He suddenly lifted her gently away from him, breathing rapidly as was she, with her eyes half closed.

Always a Romance of Lemuria

"Until the day after tomorrow, which is already tomorrow," he said, his black eyes shining with that passion yet tenderness that only he could combine of all the men she'd ever seen in life or dreams.

"Anything worth having is worth waiting for, though it may be aeons of time so tomorrow is but a second in the scheme of destiny!" Reluctantly she cast her eyes down, he was right, hard though it would be, it was but a second in ages of time, as he said, and in their time of waiting it was indeed even less of a second to wait for love's fulfilment!

He took his jacket off and put it around her shoulders and picking her up in his arms, strode through the main living room which was in darkness and through the French windows, down terrace steps along tree lined walks, then through a gate which opened onto more steps which led down to the beach.

Here he set her down and her bare feet sank into sand like silver dust in the moonlight and there was the hiss and swish of the waves on the beach.

"I think you... and I need some air, for a little while," he put his arm around her shoulders as they walked towards the surf.

"How did the other 'me' have the accident," she asked curiously.

"It was about ten days ago, we were with the location manager, she hadn't been officially signed up for the part in the film at the time, although we knew it was hers. We were looking at the beach a few miles from here. Although a lot of it is to be filmed in Hawaii, as well as the studio, Jim, who finds the locations thought the flight of steps down from the rocks to the beach would be suitable for a particular scene. I was talking to him... and... the other you started down the steps, she must have slipped or tripped, she screamed and before we could reach her, she kind of slid down the steps on her back, it had been raining, and they were very slippy. We thought she would probably injure her back, but as she came to a halt at the bottom, her head snapped back, a kind of 'whiplash' I suppose, and she banged her head and by the time we got to her, she was unconscious!

"She'd hit the back of her head although there was also a small cut on her temple which she must have scraped on the side during the fall. We got her to hospital, they said it was bad concussion, no other injuries, but she lay there in a coma just as you saw her, they were wrong she must have had some kind of haemorrhage," he clutched her to him, "oh my darling, I wanted to die, when the doctor told me she had gone, and then when I saw YOU, the other YOU with your beautiful eyes open, I thought

I was dreaming, that perhaps I HAD died and I was with you, but everything is alright now!"

"There's something else I don't understand, the other me showed you the book, but...'" he finished her sentence... "and Jenny Rainer showed it me twenty years ago... yes that's true, but had almost forgotten, it being 20 years... countless films and two wives!"

"I understand," she said, smiling up at him. "I discovered something about the writer, about a year ago in my own time, and I'd forgotten... she was something to do with a group of psychics led by a Russian woman, the writer claimed that her novel was TRUE, that she was re-telling the story of two lovers, one who had been the Queen of Lemuria... do you think that we were these Lovers?"

"I think that perhaps we were, although I didn't know about the author... it's possible!"

"But why aren't you in my own time?" she said, pressing herself close, "as someone else?"

"I'm going to die, aren't I?" he said gently. She looked down. "I just can't remember, truly I can't remember" she looked up at him.

"It doesn't matter, that's why you've come back to me, perhaps time made an error, they say no-one is ever cheated, for whatever reason this is happening, it will turn out alright, we've found each other and will again.

Love is eternal, and somehow I know whatever we missed in those other lives will be given back and it will be for always!" He tried to make light conversation as they walked hand in hand. He began asking about his fellow stars, what had happened to them, if they still lived.

Lunaflora looked at him mischievously... "if you're asking me about your ex-wives, as far as I know they are still living, Marta Helman for sure." He looked at her with amusement...

"And Jenny Rainer and er... etc?'"

"They will all live out their span," she said with a low laugh.

"And what about the male stars, Jimmy Stewart for instance?"

"Jimmy Stewart has had, a long, in fact he's had a WONDERFUL LIFE!" Tristan laughed.

"I'm glad... a great guy!"

"Oh... and one will become, late in life, President of the United States!" He looked at her in genuine amazement.

"No kidding?"

"No kidding... and for TWO terms!"

"Who?"

"That's funny, I can't remember, yet I can see his warm smile and very blue eyes. I really can't remember, it's as if something is preventing me from remembering!"

"Well, never mind, perhaps I'm not meant to know, though I could make a good guess!"

She found the same thing happened when asked about others, mainly those she knew were no longer alive.

"We will return to the house for the moment," he said gently, but still gazing at Lunaflora with great passion, so that it gave the girl almost a kind of physical pain in her fast beating heart as if a sharp knife was slowly being pushed through her body, right through her heart, yet so exquisite that it almost made her fall and he caught her in his arms as she went off balance.

"Are you alright sweetheart," he whispered in a husky voice.

"Yes... yes," she answered, unable to meet his eyes. They walked slowly back to the house, their intertwined figures casting fantastic and mysterious shadows on the moonlit beach, the surf pounding only a few feet away as it must have done through untold ages of time and their eternal love, that pounded with those untold ages in time with the surf pounding the beaches of a mighty continent swallowed by the ocean long ago, and the present land where that other self had died. All these thoughts ran through her head as Tristan walked very close beside her, his arm gripping her waist like a vice, yet with a gentleness that intoxicated the very stuff of her Being!"

Chapter Eight

Lunaflora slept late the following morning, when Mrs Lawson, Tristan's housekeeper, (who she just remembered in time, she was supposed to have met before) came to wake her with a 'late breakfast'. It was already near midday. Tristan, she was told had gone to the studio early.

"I'll come back and run your bath my dear," said the cheerful, elderly woman.

"Thank you, Mrs Lawson," said Lunaflora, looking through the open window at the blue Pacific... suddenly... the sea darkened... and she saw The City... the city shone like gold, Lunaflora realized it WAS gold, the palace, the great Temple were all coated with solid gold, silver and some red shining unknown metal at the base of the pyramid shaped buildings. The tops of the high towers were made of the deepest pink coral, and the colours blazed in the setting sun. In the palace garden, were trees with branches, leaves, blossoms and fruit made of pure gold and silver, the red roses were formed of real rubies and the eight foot high violets were of the deepest violet coloured amethysts she had ever seen, though she preferred the natural plants, this artificial garden was the work of master craftsmen and designed by an undoubtedly great artist!... the girl blinked... the vision of golden turrets disappeared, there were only the waves of the high noon Pacific again... and the housekeeper called from the beautiful bathroom. Lunaflora saw the kind of real bath foam that one only usually sees in films. The housekeeper went out and shut the door.

Lunaflora lowered herself into the bath, even the foam was the colour of the moonflower. She pulled her hair loose and her long golden tresses floated like a mermaid's in the perfumed water. She jumped up and down like a child in a swimming pool and then gave a yelp of surprise as the door opened and Tristan peered around the door! She huddled down in the foam, her face a very bright pink. He gave a mischievous grin...

"Don't worry, I won't look, much as I'd like to!!... but I have something exciting to tell you when you're decent," and he laughed and closed the door, leaving a very pink mermaid, her blood pounding, but not from schoolgirl modestly! Later, after she had chosen a pink blouse and a full white fifties style skirt from the vast wardrobe and finding some somewhat cumbersome but white lacy basic underwear with numerous petticoats to put on first, after all, her own clothes had disappeared, they were in a hotel bedroom 35 years in the future, a pair of white sandals completed the outfit and she brushed out her still slightly damp hair and tied it with a pink ribbon in a ponytail, a style popular in the fifties and in her own time. Lunch was set out on a table on the terrace. Tristan stood there, wearing a white open necked shirt and beige slacks which did justice to the California tan which darkened his naturally pale skin, as his complexion, even though his hair and eyes were so dark was not of the olive kind, but a legacy of the fair skin of his English father. His beauty stabbed her anew. He pulled out a chair so that she could see over the garden.

"Ma belle," he whispered as she sat down. For the first time she saw the swimming pool below, like her bath, flower shaped, but lined with tiles of forget-me-not blue. They ate in silence, with only the swishing sound of the ocean and the cry of the gulls. When they were drinking coffee, Tristan stood up and lit a cigarette, and showed Lunaflora the lighter the other 'girl' had given him.

"Toujours," she read.

"Ah," he whispered, "you both speak French!"

"Yes, I speak French and I guessed the other me also spoke it!"

He was fascinated by descriptions of life in the future, the new technology, and in particular, the kind of movies they made, and television and videos. His quick intelligence grasped the principles of the end products of things that had only been little more than ideas, or in their infancy in his time, things he might have seen, they both realized, had he lived!

"But I'd be awful old!" He laughed. She looked up at him.

"There's a saying that no-one is old until there is no-one left to remember them when they were young, and your films are still being shown, so even without this fantastic time shift, you'll always be young!" He stared at his cigarette, her eyes following the graceful movement of his elegant hands, hands that sent a wave of heat through her body until it reached her head, which thumped until the rising passion almost choked her. She pretended the coffee caused her to splutter, he was beside her in a second...

"Are you OK?" She raised her eyes to his, "yes, the coffee went the wrong way," but her face betrayed her, and the devilish look in his eyes told her he was not deceived. He tipped her back in his arms and plundered her lips with a kiss that she returned with equal passion and yet surrender. Then he drew away and stood with his back to the terrace.

"Darling," he said softly in that low, seductive voice... the word and the voice travelling to her nerve endings with an almost physical pain of heady sweetness and excitement.

"I thought this was to be our secret wedding day as I am now legally free of Conchita," he enunciated the name with a contemptuous reluctance and filled Lunaflora with a pang of jealousy, though unnecessary, jealousy that was a bottomless void, for that woman had at least experienced physically, that which Lunaflora was desperate to give and receive, for which she had waited a lifetime and now was about to be thwarted again. Her face paled. She looked at the shining depthless blackness of those eyes which seemed to read her every thought.

"It will happen my love, just be patient a little longer," his lips whispered against her cheek.

"My future self has never... " she began shyly.

"I can tell that pichina," using the Italian for 'little girl'.

"Yet I'm really ten years older than the 'me' you knew before."

"It doesn't matter, you could be 18, don't you realise how beautiful you are, how exciting and desirable, yet with that untouched look and a modesty that is more alluring than all the sophisticated brazenness of my so-called lady friends!" She blushed. He placed the half finished cigarette on an ashtray.

"No, I'm afraid the postponement is film business. The studio bosses have seen your screen test but they haven't met YOU. Your contract is signed for 'Always' and work will begin almost immediately, most of it will be filmed in Hawaii, oh it's beautiful there! Well, the point is, that Boris Varrak, the head of Romulus 2000 is holding a big reception this evening at his home in the Hollywood hills, and he wants to see YOU, it's nothing to worry about, just choose a beautiful dress and make yourself even more beautiful... if that's possible" he said with a lingering glance. "We'll have dinner here before we go, because you'll only get cocktails and small morsels of nothing on little sticks when you are at the party."

Later that afternoon, as the honey coloured sun sank low on a liquid gold horizon where fairy tale dream-like towers may once have soared into the deepening blue of night, Lunaflora rose from her bed where she had slept for a few hours, her heart beating with trepidation at the prospect of the evening's ordeal. Tristan had gone out, so she drank more milk and ate a slice of cake which the housekeeper had left beside the bed.

Then once again, after undressing, she walked to the bathroom, and once more sank into the bath foam, once more letting her golden hair, which had already been made a little more gold by the strong sunlight, float in the water. She floated, perhaps as she had done in a beautiful lake, thousands of years ago, with only the sound of a waterfall and the silence of a still young world.

By the time she had finished bathing, it was already dark. She went into the dressing room which led out of the bedroom and wondered what on earth she should wear... Tristan would know, but he would not be back until it was almost time for the reception... and if she asked the housekeeper, she would think it was strange. She looked at the beautiful evening dresses and tried to visualise images of fifties fashions in films she had seen.

At last she selected a beautiful cream silk gown, ankle length, then searched for suitable underwear. She found it in a drawer and stared with horror at the constricting brassieres of the fifties and equally tight girdles! Although in her own time stockings had come back into fashion for young and older women, Lunaflora scorned them, sticking to the tights of her generation... but there was no pantyhose here! In the end, studying her slim figure in the mirror, she decided to risk wearing the gown with only a pair of frilly pants beneath. Her long slim legs were flawless, and it was a long skirt... She put on the gown, a perfect fit... the dress had puffed sleeves, and a low neckline, slightly off the shoulder, and it revealed a lot of white bosom. She found some matching high heeled cream sandals, also a perfect fit and under the lights the opalescent moonflower motifs on the gown sparkled. In a drawer she found an evening bag, again shaped just like a moonflower with a silver chain. She then opened the jewel case and took out the moonflower necklace, the matching earrings and bracelet and flower for her hair which still hung damply down her back.

She found a small waterproof cape which she placed around her shoulders and stretched a wide headband over her forehead to keep her hair back and then studied the cosmetics. She saw the rather heavy powder and paints of the fifties, and lipsticks of more limited colours than the nineties. In a small cream velvet bag she found a gold powder compact, again shaped like a moonflower and studded with opals. Inside was a powder puff and old fashioned loose face powder, someone had used it at least once!... her other self, no doubt, and the powder was the exact shade of her own complexion. She decided to... as far as possible, make up as she would in her own time. She stared critically at her face in the mirror. She had a perfect skin. It was of the translucent paleness that only the English possess. As a child, there had been the bloom of the rose, but it had faded to the hue of a creamy white pearl in adulthood. She put a dusting of the powder from the compact over her face, then searching for the blusher or rouge as it was then called, she applied some pale pink lightly high on her cheekbones, then set it with another dusting of powder. She disdained foundation in this time or her own. Then she stared at her eyes, large, dark grey-blue ones, long lashes and unusually for a blonde, dark, well shaped eyebrows! She took up a stick of kohl or what passed for eyeliner and, as she always did, outlined her eyes beneath the lower lashes extending the line beyond the corner of her eyes 'a la Cleopatra'. She then found some old fashioned mascara in a little box which she remembered to spit on and moistened a small brush and applied it to her upper lashes, so long, they looked as good as false ones.

She then darkened her eyebrows a little more with an eyebrow pencil. Finally she found a lipstick and a gold case, the colour of a dark red rose, and applied it to her full but prettily shaped lips.

She then removed the cape and the hair band and picked up hairbrush and brushed her golden hair until, it crackled with electricity, flew out and settled into a shining cascade down her back and around her shoulders. She then carefully placed the flower clip, holding back the hair, just below the temple and put on the matching earrings, necklace, and bracelet. She sprayed some perfume... 'Fleur de la Lune' on her neck, ears and wrists, pushed the lipstick and compact into her evening bag, stepped back and looked in the mirror. Her skirts belled out like a flower and petals clung to the body of the shining, stunning blonde and fairy tale princess beauty of the reflection... that she could hardly believe was herself... Lunaflora!

Always a Romance of Lemuria

She came out of the trance when she heard the voice that never failed to make her heart skip a thousand beats call her name from the hallway. She took a deep breath, and pulling the matching cream stole around her shoulders, walked along the landing and stood at the head of the staircase, and started to walk down towards the beautiful male vision in immaculate black evening dress who stood... transfixed... his long lashed brilliant black eyes shining with desire! Part of herself almost laughed with triumph and slight amusement, how many times had she watched him in just such a scene in his many films, watching the beautiful heroine coming down the staircase, only this was for REAL and the desire that she saw in his eyes, that made her dizzy...was for her.

As she started down the stair, she raised her eyes to the wall opposite the stair head and for a frozen moment in time was transfixed by the full length portrait which almost touched the ceiling and covered most of the wall space. In its huge gilt frame, was an original oil painting, in the style of an artist such as Van Dyke... a portrait of Tristan on a rearing black horse... he... dressed as a cavalier... completely in black, plumed hat, long black curled hair and raised sword, a black mask concealing his flashing dark eyes! It was Tristan in his most famous swashbuckling role... 'The Black Cavalier'... where his wonderful swordsmanship had been the most spectacular. It was loosely based on the life of a real life 17th century French highwayman... Claude Duval who had reached an untimely end in England, remembered mainly for his gallantry to the ladies! In the film, he had been re-invented as a friend of the exiled King Charles II, vanquishing his enemies and helping him to regain his throne... a masked crusader... falling in love with Charles' youngest sister, Minette (who married the brother of Louis XIIII of France), played in the film by the exquisitely beautiful, dark eyed young actress, Belinda Daniels, who a few years later was tragically killed in the blitz while in London. Minette dies... and Claude dies too, and at the end of the film it shows his tombstone (which really existed, and with the same inscription... minus 'The Black Cavalier') 'Here lies Claude Duval... Gentleman... and Highwayman... if reader male thou be... look to thy purse... but if thou be female... look to thy heart!... end of film!

She came out of her trance and gazed in adoration at her beloved cavalier as she continued down the staircase. When she reached the bottom stair, he said in that soft, deep voice, with a trace of huskiness...

"Shall we go Princess?" She managed to look up into his eyes, but she was strangely shy.

"Yes," she whispered. She took his arm and they went outside to the waiting limousine and this time he sat in the back with her, slipping his arm around her waist, but gently, allowing for her beautiful gown... could he feel her heart beating?... How she longed for him to take her in his arms, but she just felt the slight jolt of the car as it drove up the twisting road into the Hollywood hills. The higher they went she saw the stars coming closer, seeming to dip towards the dark sea and land, then up to the heavens again with the movement of the car, until it almost made her dizzy and a little sick, as the dinner that had been promised had not materialised due to Tristan's late homecoming. The lights of an oncoming car lit up her pale face and Tristan said anxiously...

"Are you unwell?"

"I just feel a little sick, it's the bends of the road and no food, I always did suffer from road and sea sickness!"

"Take a deep breath and close your eyes, that was thoughtless of me, I should have made sure you ate something, but never mind, I'll ask for something, we'll soon be there... lean against me," he said gently. She leant gratefully against his shoulder and closed her eyes, in a kind of peace as the turmoil, inside and out, fled away!

At last they turned into a steep twisting driveway, dark trees forming an archway overhead like a natural cathedral, open to the sky. Eventually the car stopped before a large gothic style mansion, mixed strangely with other styles... a hodge podge of lighted windows and illuminated turrets. The chauffeur opened the door for them and Tristan helped Lunaflora out, their feet crunching on gravel. An imposing carved wooden door stood open where the host's English butler stood stiffly to usher them in.

Tristan, completely at his ease, slapped the man's shoulder in a friendly but obviously humorous fashion, deflating the butler's poker faced pomposity.

"'How are you Brown, old friend?" he asked with a flash of mischief in his dark eyes.

"Very well sir," the man replied stiffly, and showed them through into a crowded reception room... Lunaflora, somewhat dazed, seemed to see hundreds of people with hundreds of raucous voices to match, nearly all the women with diamonds flashing at their throats, ears, wrists, fingers, and even on their gowns! As Lunaflora entered there was a sudden silence... the women distinctly unfriendly as their male companions surged forward to crowd around Lunaflora. She was vaguely aware of whispers...

"Who IS this gorgeous creature?... trust Tristan to bring an exotic flower to put all the weeds to shame!" Tristan just laughed and holding the girl tightly around her shoulders, took her through to a conservatory, where among the real exotic plants and palms was a comfortable cushioned wicker chair with a high, fan shaped back.

He snapped an order to a nearby waiter and within five minutes, he and Lunaflora were consuming chicken sandwiches accompanied by the finest champagne. After eating several of the sandwiches and a glass of champagne, Lunaflora began to feel better. Tristan leaned towards her.

"Better... Darling?" he asked.

"Yes, much," she answered quietly, blushing at the sudden use of that particular endearment. There was a loud 'meow', and looking down she saw a large tabby cat with wide green eyes, staring at her and at the chicken, and as she stared into those green eyes, she saw her own beautiful cat, Caruso, against the background of misty English fields, and as so often she related her feelings to songs... a snatch of 'mists of England, standing on a hill... I remember this... and I always will!' from 'Hello Young Lovers' went through her head and she suddenly felt a great pang of homesickness and yearning for her beloved pet and land, run through her like a silent cry and she knew that sometime she would have to return... and part of her wanted to... had to... in spite of her love for the beautiful man who looked at her with concern...

"What is it?" he asked.

"The cat," she began... "he made me think of my own cat and home!"

"Ah... I see," he said, a little wistfully, "that's understandable, you belong to the future whatever you feel for me... and belong to England... but whatever happens Darling, I'll always be with you, we'll find each other again... and I too spring... in a sense, through my father, from the same soft mists of England." She stared back at him, he might have read her thoughts. The cat decided to jump onto her lap, purring, elegantly seizing a piece of chicken with his paw and directing it directly into his mouth.

"This is Buttons, mine host's pampered pet," Tristan informed her, "as you love cats, mine host will be putty in your hands!" The cat licked a paw, then stared at Lunaflora intently again, and this time, the reflection in his eyes was a pyramid shaped temple, shining with layers of pure gold, with little turrets from where dozens of golden bells rang with silver chimes amid waving palm trees... she blinked the cat wore a yellow collar with tiny gold bells all around which tinkled as he washed himself. Suddenly she was aware of the perfume of exotic plants in the conservatory, particularly the overpowering scent of an enormous violet that she seemed to recall in a dream, the cat seemed to take on the look of another kind of cat, the same, yet different from an older world, somewhere between that of the Egyptian feline and a small wild cat. Its eyes were enormous, like shining emeralds, hypnotizing her, and it

Always a Romance of Lemuria

suddenly jumped up and... startled... she leaned towards Tristan and she was hypnotized again by the dark fiery passion of his eyes, and again, as if those same eyes had been in another world, and he suddenly pulled her to him until she lay across him, he, supporting her head as his eyes came closer as he bent his own dark head, mingling with her golden hair as his mouth ravished her parted lips with a passion that made her senses reel and she arched her body, feeling a sensuous scorching heat, and a yearning primitive desire to give herself completely to this beautiful and most beloved of men!

The rest of that evening passed as a dream within a dream, after that moment of passion, she only felt real, though dizzy with desire as he waltzed with her around the shining dance floor, held close in his arms, as she had always wanted to be when she had watched his elegant dancing on a flickering screen, it was at last real, it must be, only something real could feel like this, like flying through the air, not dancing!

All the women watched with malevolence and jealousy, she was introduced to the stereotype of the studio boss, with the inevitable cigar that made her cough, one however, of the few heads of studios in the whole of Hollywood who was an intellectual and in fact had originally been a serious writer coming into the movie business through the medium of writing screenplays. No surprise then, that though a commercial studio, whose target was the box office, this particular studio head mixed commercial material with adaptations to the screen of the work of the best English and American writers of the twentieth century, a good example being 'The Eye of a Needle', probably the most intellectual role Tristan ever had the opportunity of playing, taken from the novel of a distinguished and almost legendary English novelist who knew Tristan personally and always insisted that he had had Tristan in mind for his character when the screen adaptation was first broached.

All these thoughts ran through Lunaflora's mind as she smiled and nodded like an animated doll to the many people at that reception, inwardly noting with amusements the 'false bonhomie' that Hollywood people were famous for, that she had read about but never thought to experience at first hand, particularly, the hateful envy behind the smiles of nearly all the women there, but all through it she was aware of Tristan's strong and loving arm around her shoulder, like a shield of protection and love between her shining spirit and the gaudy glitter that hid a pack of human wolves. The days and months flew by in a dreamlike state as they filmed 'Always', in that time that was not hers, almost as if she was watching a film of herself with Tristan, perhaps it was a kind of dream, as if time was speeded up like the fast forward on a video recorder, to reach a certain point in the film being watched... the night they arrived back at his house after that reception, as he stood by her bedroom door, she threw herself against him in surrender, his kisses were violent in their passionate intensity, but then with an effort, he drew back.

"Dearest Lunaflora, I know that our union will come, but when the time is right, whether now or in that other life to which you must, sometime, inevitably return, but promise me one thing!"

"Anything... my darling..."' she said through wracking sobs.

He stared at her from his beautiful eyes... "if one day, in your real life and time... you look into a man's eyes, a man who perhaps you have just met, and he says... maybe this is an old line and sounds crazy, but I feel we know each other... and perhaps you'll feel the same about this man... so... promise me, you'll give him a chance, not many people get a third chance." She suddenly understood.

"You mean, it will be YOU... come back to me!"

"Yes, and we shall have found each other again and it will be for always!... will you promise to remember my dearest!"

"Oh yes... my darling... I promise... always, always," and she swayed and fainted in his arms.

When they were filming the very last sequence of 'Always', her last memory was of being held in Tristan's arms in aqua blue waters just a few yards from the glittering white sands and palm trees of a Hawaiian beach which was the location. There was no need of special effects to simulate the sudden enormous waves which seemed to come from nowhere! She saw the great wall of water coming towards them and the faint screams of the film crew... as Tristan held her tight until they were entwined... but had never been united in love, and the waiting had been in vain!... and now it was too late! She screamed with agony, not from fear of drowning, but from a broken heart... Tristan kissing her mouth in his own agony, and the last thing she remembered was his voice saying...

"Don't be afraid, I will be with you... ALWAYS!" and she, her real self, and in her own body, seemed to rise out of that other body and out of the angry waters and she saw that other Lunaflora and her beloved Tristan disappear beneath the heaving waves... then there was darkness and she knew no more!

Part Two

'Moonflower'
Queen of Lemuria
24,000 BC

'Light of my eyes
The Nightingale has returned.
We will lose ourselves in the garden
And come out in blossom
Like the lilies and the roses, we will
become water and flow
From garden to garden!
 ... Persian Poem

Chapter Nine

The High Sacred Mountain of the Lemurian Empire, overlooking the aqua blue water of ocean on three sides, rose like the faceted jewel of many colours from an enormous emerald which was the green of the forest which surrounded the base of the rocky mountain.

On the flat top of the peak were gigantic stone statues, some, 25 feet high, in seven circles, radiating outwards to the outermost circle, which unlike the others, looked out towards the sea. They had peculiar features of flattened foreheads, noses sloping outwards to the tip, and jutting lips. Their eyes were real sapphires or emeralds, and on their heads they wore strange looking top knots or hats, formed completely of bright red rubies. The outermost circle, permanently gazing across the distant land and sea, unlike the others had red rubies for eyes as well as for their hats, at certain times, at night, lighting up like a modern electrical device, so they shone as brightly as the lamp of a modern lighthouse, but multiplied many times, shining eerily, and guarding the sacred mountain!

A little lower down the mountain was a flat clearing, paved with great stones, this was the landing place for vimana aircraft, used mainly by the Indra Empire, an ancient colony of Lemuria, but now an independent state. The port could handle both small personal aircraft and the larger commercial and passenger airships from far off Atlantis, the other side of the world, Indra and Atlantis were not on friendly terms, Atlantis, though advanced in science and magic were warlike, whereas Indra though peaceful were far advanced in the power of the mind for controlling events and elements... and people... consequently these powers could be used for the purpose of defence in times of war. The more practical Atlanteans were sceptical, and laughed, thinking it was only empty boasting!... but the High Priests of Indra only smiled and kept their own counsel!

In between these two empires, in an enormous fertile valley, over two thousand square miles, and as long was the Empire of Medit, it sat almost geographically between the northern and southern hemispheres as would be understood today, and they ruled all the surrounding areas. The rulers, both equal as king and queen, were Osiyrus and Lotus, Lotus being the sister of Rama, Emperor of Indra. This state too had great powers and was, in time of war, the half way place for the meeting of the armies of Poseidon of Atlantis and Rama of Indra!

In a partly natural amphitheatre at the very top of the peak were seven seats. The three to each side of the largest, which was the throne, were of stone. On these were seated three women in elaborate robes on the right, and to the left, three men in similar robes. The throne was constructed from a solid block of coral, and on it was seated Moonflower, Queen of Lemuria, the most beautiful queen on earth! Her golden hair, blazing in the sun reached to below her knees and each strand was entwined with amber beads. On her head rested the heavy gold and silver crown with enormous luminous opals fashioned like moonflowers, their 'petals' being the points of the crown. Around her neck was a necklace of opal moonflowers which hung over her full breasts which her fabulous apparel did not hide but revealed completely! From her ears hung heavy earrings, two large opal moonflowers, her large, brilliant blue eyes were outlined with kohl and extended outwards in Egyptian style, her dark eyelashes, like thick fans, needed no enhancing. Her lips were reddened with coral coloured rouge. Her costume was suspended from a wide gold collar around her neck and shoulders and was made completely of coral and amber beads, hanging in strands from neck to waist, moving as she moved, revealing the full breasts with their coral coloured nipples. Around her hips was a golden belt with coral clasps from which hung again a heavily beaded skirt of coral and amber beads in long strands to her ankles, revealing her shapely hips and thighs. At wrists and ankles were opal bracelets. On her feet she wore coral sandals with high square heels. On her right

Always a Romance of Lemuria

hand was a large opal moonflower ring and on left she wore a coral and amber ring, shaped like a rose.

Seated at her feet, warm fur pressing fondly against her leg, was a large cat, very like a modern domestic cat, but about the size of a cheetah. He had short thick fur, light brown, with black stripes, similar to the modern tabby, and with lazy emerald eyes outlined by a black stripe which tilted upwards at the corners, in effect... a natural eyeliner! He had powerful paws and sheathed claws on which his head rested, and he wore a wide gold collar with emeralds, hollowed out into the shape of bells which tinkled in silvery chimes as he moved, making a counter melody with his loud purring. Moonflower lowered her hand and stroked his head to which he responded by rubbing her hand.

"Sphinx" (named for the great guardian statues of the temples) she whispered in a soft voice and he stared up at his mistress with love and adoration. There was a roar from the other side of the throne... she turned her head and stared into the yellow gold eyes of a small type of dragon, about the size of a Shetland pony. Bright red flame issued from his parted jaws. He was the bright green of the dragons of future legend, sharp pointed ears, shining scales, pointed ridges along the spine ending in a forked tail, four wicked looking feet with lethal claws and folded bat-like wings.

"Komoda," the girl whispered, "be silent!" He sat down, his gold collar straining on a heavy gold chain attached to an iron ring at the back of the throne. 'Sphinx' was her beloved pet.... 'Komoda'... her faithful guard... the unlikely pair rarely left her side.

She glanced across at the clearing where her personal vimana stood... shaped like an enormous swan with outstretched wings... remembered in primitive future myths as a 'magic bird', it had seating inside for twenty people, beside the pilot and co-pilot, with crystal windows set in the mother of pearl which coated its special metal bodywork... It contained areas for taking food and drink, for washing, and the relief of personal functions. For long flights, the seats could be converted to comfortable sleeping couches... and if the need arose, the pilot and co-pilot could render the aircraft invisible to those below or to other aircraft... and if really necessary could use laser weapons to completely destroy and cause the disappearance of enemy vimanas!

"Rama," Moonflower whispered, and her heart turned over as she visualised the fabulous dark beauty of her Beloved, in his golden armour... even now fighting as King of Indra in the terrible war that the aggressive Atlanteans had started in all the neighbouring empires... and if not stopped it would soon reach Lemuria! She shuddered, both for her husband-to-be and their future world! She looked up into the sky, where even in the blue of day, could be seen the largest planet in their galaxy, the Planet of Green Fire! Many times bigger than the planets the future would know as Saturn or Jupiter, it flashed in the sunlight, like a gigantic emerald suspended in the heavens! At night with the moon and stars, it shone with a strange radiance that added an eerie green tinge to the soft moon and starlight.

Moonflower stared down at the great stone statues and thought of the ceremony she would shortly start. Her mind travelled through millennia in a second of time. How often had she sat here for the same ceremony since childhood when she was crowned queen on this spot... this south eastern corner of a mighty continent and empire which was... or had been... the Motherland... master and mistress of the world... a world where the oceans and seas were fairly small... a world where it was possible to travel by land around the globe... even walk, if one was so foolhardy! A world which enjoyed a temperate climate and two harvests a year... where no-one knew want or hunger! Most of the earth's waters were solid ice, many miles deep, and piled many miles high at the north and south poles, yet sometimes she dreamed... and in that dream, she stood on the spot where she was now, but there was no mighty continent with a small ocean surrounding it... no... the statues stood on a tiny bleak island with water as far as the eye could see, no more lush vegetation, just statues staring out at the sea, most of them damaged or lying down, with a few strange looking people looking up at them as if in wonder. Sometimes she walked among them, but they did not see her, she was a lost soul in a soulless world, looking for the one she had loved... always... and sometimes he was beside her, but she could not see him, then she would wake among her silken cushions in her great bed, carved like a moonflower, with petals curving upward, and she would be weeping for she knew not what!

Chapter Ten

She looked once again at the statues, they were waiting for her command to start the ceremony, but again she hesitated. She thought of the history of these strange images. Only the Elders of the Temple of the Maker of the Universe, only they knew the whole truth, for they were the Guardians of all Knowledge and Wisdom!... but as queen, a queen who could read and write in the twenty most important languages of the empire and colonies, who understood the music of the spheres, who could sing, dance and play instruments to the universal rhythm and make sweet music from its inspiration, who understood and performed the magical arts, in a world where the most humble could understand and use what we would call telepathy, a world where the secret of anti gravity was known and used as well as other great knowledge that was of benefit to mankind, but without harming nature, such a great queen knew so much... of the history of these statues. Many millions of years before, when the Earth was a new world, with a race of physically beautiful human beings, but childlike in knowledge, strange men, who looked exactly like these statues, had come from the Red Planet, where because of a cataclysm, the atmosphere and environment were dying, so the few survivors, all men, had come in their airships to earth. They had chosen wives from the beautiful earth females, whose offspring, in time, grew into a new race. They taught mankind knowledge, of the Universal Creator and the ways of civilisation. Later generations had made statues of these original people.

Those original people from the Red Planet had been able to live, with the aid of their magical arts for thousands of years, then when eventually they went to their Maker, their knowledge was left in the safe hands of the elite priests who came after them. This mountain was the spot where they had first landed on earth, from their dying planet... hence the statues in their memory! Lemuria was the first civilisation on earth and from almost the beginning they had had only beautiful queens with long golden hair! Not that fair haired people were unusual, all shades of hair and skin colour, according to racial type could be found in Atlantis and other parts, but here in Lemuria... and Indra, where everyone had black hair, brown eyes and skin tones ranging from white to reddish brown, blonde hair was unique. When the Red Ones were still on earth, the earth's Moon was a small planet, with seas and verdant land, but everything was the colour of silver... and here the silver people lived, all with varying shades of blonde or auburn hair. They landed in Lemuria from their spacecraft, which was also amphibious, it could travel underwater also, it was shaped like an enormous silver dolphin. The Lemurians and other people of earth had 'submarines' too, but shaped like fish (in later ages... a man called Jonah... in legend... was swallowed by a whale... in reality he simply entered an Atlantean submarine... which was shaped like a whale!) The Silver People from the Moon were entertained by the Lemurians and when they returned to their home, they left behind the Moonflower plant, which grew in their world, and a golden haired girl baby to be the first Queen of Lemuria, and so it was that though each queen married a black haired prince, they always produced just one golden haired, blue eyed daughter to be the next queen and they were always called 'Moonflower'. All this the present queen thought of as she prepared for the ceremony. She at last gave the signal. The High Priest stood, raised his arms, and muttered certain secret words. Suddenly the statues were animated, for indeed, they were (though advanced beyond the imagination and intelligence of modern man) basically robots. They stepped off their platforms and in procession walked around the perimeter of the hill seven times in time to a beautiful melody which seemed to come from out of the air... then they again took up their positions on the platforms and were still again... just statues.

The significance of the ceremony was virtually lost, except by the priests, but was meant to ensure the safety and prosperity of Lemuria! Moonflower smiled grimly to herself as she re-entered her swan aircraft to return to her northern capital of Haviki, over 2000 miles away, but reached in 10 minutes, such was the speed of the aircraft. The pilot reported grave news about the war in Indra.

"Show me," commanded Moonflower, her heart beating in panic.

In the salon they uncovered a large globe of clear crystal, Moonflower stared into it... when the mists cleared, she saw her beloved... Rama, in his golden armour, seated on his beautiful white war horse at the scene of battle.

His beautiful voice rang out from the globe... "Moonflower... my beloved...." he began, and unfolded the terrible events that had taken place at his capital while he had been fighting elsewhere. The Atlanteans had seized all the empires between their land and Indra, including Merit, whose armies had failed to check the enemy... They were also in control of Teewanaka, the enormous continent which stretched from the north to the south pole and was joined, on the west, to Lemuria, in short, they were nearly the masters of the earth. Moonflower felt perspiration break out on her forehead... fear? At a time when the earth was perfectly upright on its axis...

where the rate of its spinning was much slower, on its own, and its journey around the sun, the climate was temperate all over the earth, with lush vegetation, in what were later arctic and Antarctic wastes were mild climates and coral reefs in the shallow oceans, where herds of mammoths, mastodons, and other such animals grazed in peace. There were no seasons as we know them now, no storms, no tornados, little rain, the morning vapour like mists watered a verdant earth which was indeed an earthly paradise. Their day was 30 hours long, not 24, and night time darkness was short, no- one needed as much sleep, though that was a matter of choice! The planets were all in harmony, the earth, if not the people, were perfect, but all that was about to change! Had not the priests and astronomers who were one and the same reported some strange explosion in the heavens? Was it a judgment by the eternal? Rama continued... in Rama's capital of Hadeeja, the Atlantean armies had assembled on the plain outside the high city walls. Rama's High Priest, an aged man and ancient in wisdom and secret magical powers, though it was not really magic, just power harnessed by their knowledge, stood on the battlements and confronted them, and told them that if they did not retreat and return from whence they had come, he would cause all the leaders and main ranks to fall dead! The Atlantean generals had only laughed and jeered, so the

High Priest raised his hands and merely stared at them... they no longer laughed, they clutched their chests in agony and literally did fall dead! The rest of the army ran away in fear and amazement... so the city was saved but only for the moment... the incident had only enraged the Atlantean Emperor, and their new army advanced on Hadeeja and used the long forbidden atom bolt, the most deadly weapon ever invented, not used since they had had to destroy the enormous dinosaurs who would have destroyed mankind a hundred thousand years ago! Now it was being used again, the mushroom clouds were seen from hundreds of miles away... millions of burned corpses of people and animals lay everywhere, the once verdant land was black with burning and smoke, the rivers ran red, survivors plunged into the water in their agony, suffering from the radioactive fallout, whole cities lay silent, and the dead lay in the streets, some embracing, women, children. There was darkness and pollution in the skies, not only in Indra, but everywhere, every shred of land was destroyed from the north to the south pole, except in Lemuria and Atlantis! Lemuria would be the next target!... all this Rama reported... then he ended, saying,

"I will return to you, my Beloved, we will defeat them, they CAN yet be defeated and then we will marry!"

Moonflower shuddered as the picture faded, and tears ran down her face... Rama joined his armies with those of Lemuria and other remaining allies and they eventually did defeat the Atlanteans, but the war was fought all over the earth and there was no spot other than in the country of the enemy and Lemuria that was not destroyed by the atom bolt, though even the sacred mountain in the extreme south east of Lemuria did not escape some burning!

In the great hall of the Palace in Lemuria's capital of Haviki, the marble hall and columns were decorated in fantastic patterns of flowers made of coral, green jade, rubies, emeralds and opals, and in between the columns, giant sized statues of goddesses stood or reclined, in a world where humans and every living thing was much taller and bigger, the statues were indeed giants. Moonflowers and other blossoms twisted themselves around the columns and statues, growing inward from the open terraces from which came a cooling breeze. Lemurs climbed up the greenery on the columns surveying the scene below with huge curious eyes.

Here Moonflower held court seated on her moonflower shaped throne, made of silver, gold and opals. She was dressed in a gown sewn with real moonflowers on cool white silk, mixed in with opal moonflowers, and her golden hair braided with pearls, her opal moonflower crown on her golden head. The most wonderful singer in the world was singing a love song to her and her beloved Rama, who stood at her side, now dressed in white with gold sandals, arm bands, and golden circlet on his thick black hair. They had just, at last, been married, and this was their wedding feast entertainment. Why were they happy, thought Moonflower when most of the earth is destroyed and it would take years to put to rights... even with their knowledge! But as she exchanged a shy glance with Rama... surely to love was to be happy?... whatever the outcome. This wedding day was her crowning glory, her husband's arm was around her shoulders, and fulfilment of love and passion was at last in sight. She had never seen or heard this singer before, yet his voice, and person, were familiar, powerful body, dark hair and flashing eyes, and a voice that was a gift of the Eternal. He too sang to the music of the spheres and could make the spirits of the air weep! It was fifteen of the clock, midday in a world of a 30 hour day, night was brief and when that brief darkness descended, Rama carried Moonflower to the waterfall in the Valley of the Moonflowers, where naked, they entered the beautiful pool surrounded by violets and moonflowers with their overpowering perfume. There they embraced with total passion, then, pausing in their kisses, they looked upwards, for they had heard a mighty boom, and they saw the Planet of Green Fire explode as something crashed into it with the light of a billion suns and the earth shook as the rogue star approached their world. The last thing Moonflower remembered was a wall of water a hundred miles wide crashing over the land, and the lovers, entwined in each other's arms, never now to be united in love, only in death, sank beneath the water, Rama kissing her mouth as he whispered "Don't be afraid, my darling, I will be with you... ALWAYS..." and the darkness claimed them!

1990

Lunaflora awoke sobbing, kneeling at the feet of the angel on the grave and as the girl's eyes cleared, the angel seemed to be smiling compassionately... "please don't cry, don't be afraid," said a familiar voice, and strong arms lifted her to her feet, and someone wiped her eyes with a silk handkerchief. Where was she? She was back by the grave in her own time. Had she fallen asleep and dreamed it all? She opened her eyes wide and stared at her rescuer, no it couldn't be, was she still dreaming? Tristan stood over her.

"Tristan!" she gasped. A young man stood there who looked and sounded exactly like Tristan but who wore a smart suit of her own era.

"Lunaflora, I knew I would find you here, I understand how you feel, maybe this sounds crazy, but" ...and he was almost smiling, "haven't we met before?" Her heart pounded. What had Tristan said... if one day someone says to you... have we met before... give him a chance!

"I believe we have met before,'" she said, taking his hand, "but who are you?"

"I'm Tristan Zennor Ravenna, Tristan Zennor was my uncle," oh, now she understood.

"I think we've always known each other," he said with the same heart stopping smile. Then she fainted in his arms...

When she at last woke up, she was lying in a bed that seemed familiar, a warm breeze blew through the open window with the tang of the sea. She remembered finding herself back at the grave, weeping and almost falling into the arms of... Tristan... or at least someone who was exactly like Tristan, who had said the very same words that Tristan had predicted someone would say to her and the new Tristan seemed to know, seemed to have experienced all the same things! She suddenly sat up, this had been her bedroom in Tristan's house... but in another time... what time was this? She looked down at her clothes, she even wore the same lovely blue nightgown and hair ribbon that she had worn back in that other time. At the bottom of the bed was the beautiful Hawaiian doll with the beautiful necklace that Tristan had given her. She pulled it to her and pressed it against her. All the other things in the room were the same, the dolls, the stuffed animals, the books. Was she lost in time? The house was the same. Then she noticed a small calendar on the bedside table... 1990! So she had come back from her voyage through time and space and she remembered her time as Queen of Lemuria, she shuddered at the memory.

She heard the sound of the door opening... the other Tristan stood with a still beautiful elderly woman, the image of Tristan... she learned later that the woman's abundant black hair, worn in a plaited coronet around her head was still naturally black, no tint! The woman came to the bed and smiled kindly at Lunaflora.

"I am Francesca, Tristan's youngest sister, this Tristan is my son. This house, which thankfully, is still isolated, because my brother had the foresight to buy all the surrounding land, was left to me and now it is my son's. My older sister Maria, died long ago and so did my husband. You are incredibly like the woman my brother loved, she was so beautiful,

"You met her?" Lunaflora asked.

"Just once, when she first arrived in Hollywood, it was so tragic!" Then she looked from the girl to her son, puzzled, yet almost as if she knew.

"God moves in mysterious ways, they say no-one is ever really cheated... but I'll leave you now," and she went from the room, shutting the door. Lunaflora stared into the beautiful black eyes of the other Tristan. It was incredible, he looked exactly the same, his voice, his walk... everything! Her heart beat faster.

"You must think I'm crazy," she whispered. He gave that devastating smile.

"Then I must be crazy too... I too have dreamed and travelled in time, I know what you know!"

"Are you the same Tristan?"

"I think I must be, but it's said that nothing is impossible if you love someone enough... even miracles!... and you must give everything in order to get everything... and I think we have found each other again... and tomorrow... will you marry me... my beloved?"

She looked at him... "oh yes, my darling," and he gathered her in his arms and kissed her as she remembered. When he gently released her, he picked something up from the floor and placed them on the bed. It was a bouquet of red roses with the dew still on them... and... in emerald green fur fabric, shiny scales, pointed ears, gold eyes, forklike tail, orange 'fabric fire' around its open mouth with fabric teeth, complete with gold collar was a three foot high toy version of the real dragon which she once owned as queen of Lemuria. She picked it up by its folded bat like wings... "Komoda," she whispered, "so you remember?"

"Everything, sweetheart, and I also remember that your beautiful moonflower gown and jewellery which match the ring on your finger are still waiting for you in your dressing room... tomorrow that gown will be your bridal gown... then sweetheart... a honeymoon in Hawaii... there is a valley there with violets and moonflowers and a waterfall, maybe a little like another... in another time... and we will go there, you and I... me and my beautiful Moonflower bride... and there..." and he laughed in that familiar seductive way, and she blushed as red as the roses which he put in her arms, and then he pulled her to him, roses, dragon and all, and put his lips to hers... "and there we will fulfil our love... and maybe a little moonflower who will be called Moonflower will result from that love... and this time, my dearest dear... our love really will be for... ALWAYS!

Other Books by the Victoria Helen Turner:
When the Sun Rose in the West
Star Crystal - Daughter of Snow White, and Other Stories

Printed in the United Kingdom by
Lightning Source UK Ltd., Milton Keynes
138433UK00001B/56/P